Green
CATHEDRAL

DEE CAREY

Green Cathedral
Copyright © 2023 by Dee Carey

ISBN:
Paperback: 978-1639457489
ebook: 978-1639457496

All rights reserved. No part of this publication may be reproduced, distributed, or transmitted in any form or by any means, including photocopying, recording, or other electronic or mechanical methods, without the prior written permission of the publisher, except in the case brief quotations embodied in critical reviews and other noncommercial uses permitted by copyright law.

The views expressed in this book are solely those of the author and do not necessarily reflect the views of the publisher, and the publisher hereby disclaims any responsibility for them.

Writers' Branding
1-800-608-6550
www.writersbranding.com
media@writersbranding.com

Contents

Acknowledgements vii
Prologue ix
Chapter 1 1
Chapter 2 19
Chapter 3 29
Chapter 4 37
Chapter 5 41
Chapter 6 49
Epilogue 73

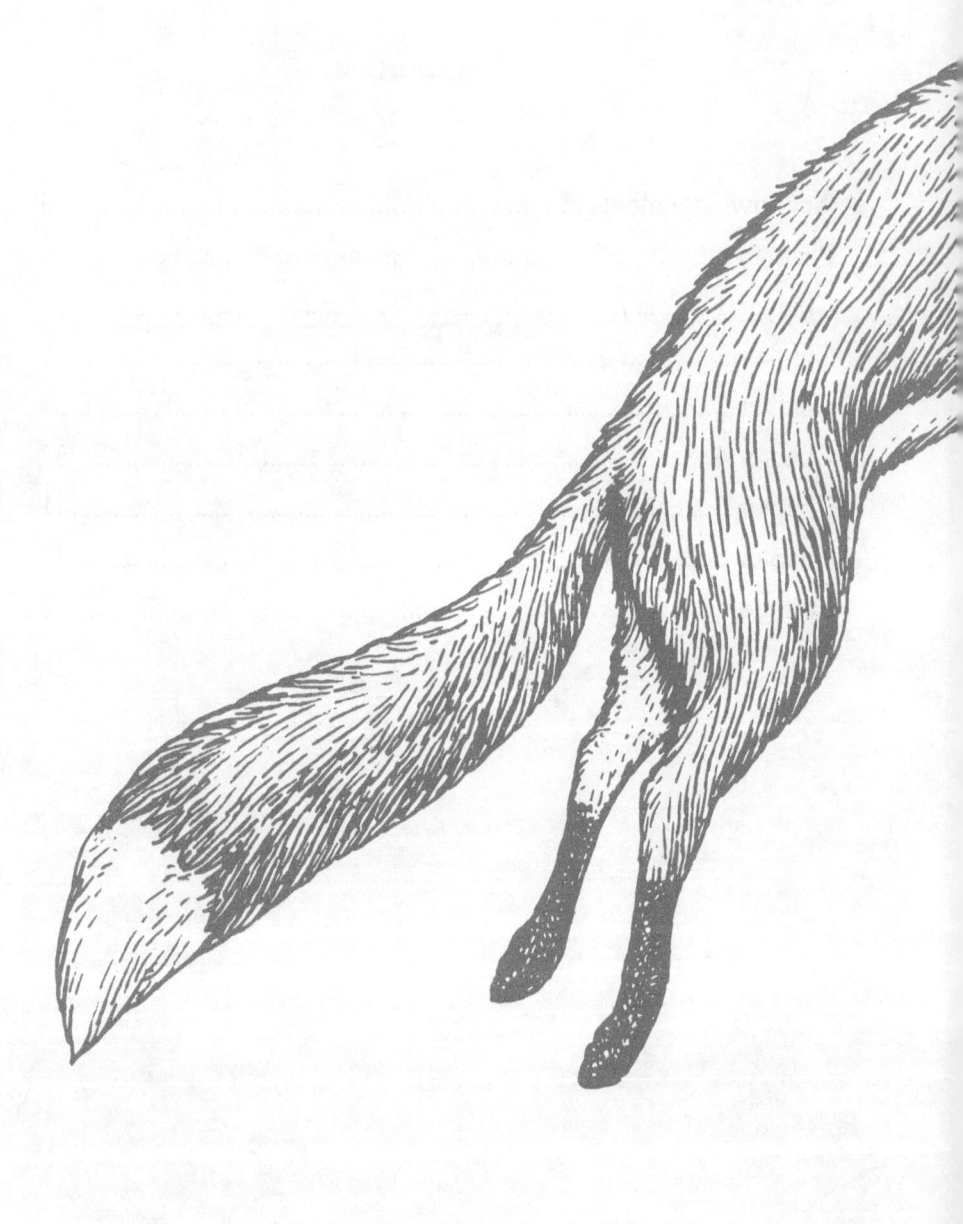

To my late husband, Bill.

To my children, Casey and Kelly.

To my grandchildren, Nik and Bill.

Acknowledgements

With deepest thanks to my amazing critique partner, Steve Yates. Without him . . . No Fox Tales.

Cast Of Characters

Lila – Third Sentinel

Reynard – Knight/ fox / Second Sentinel

Amadeaus – Druid First Sentinel

Natheria – minion of the Devil

Guinevere – King Arthur's queen

Sir Bors – Knight of the Round Table

Lady Clare – Lady-in-waiting to the Queen

King Arthur- King of Briton

Officer Neeley - head of Reynard's men

Sir Percival – A misguided knight of King Arthur's

Prologue

The sun shone through the stately pines illuminating the needles and leaves on the forest floor turning them to gold. The wood was home to a natural church. Before the altar of a fallen oak stood a massive stone cross, branches of nearby trees formed an arch above it. A sense of peace always permeated the sanctuary. It was a haven, a place to be protected for its serenity.

It was here the Ancient Order of the Tara Protectum determined would be the cornerstone church. King Arthur as a gift to his wife Guinevere commissioned the Tara Protectum to find a suitable local. So ancient the placement of the cross could not be recalled, nor could the origin of the center stone, a brilliant emerald, be remembered. It was larger than any emerald that had ever been mined. No one knew of its origin. It simply existed, and it was the duty of the Tara Protectum to preserve this Green Cathedral. It was determined a guardian would be selected to remain within the confines of the cathedral to protect both the land and the church within it. A wandering Druid priest was appointed the first Sentinel.

As men are not all noble. Certain protections were placed upon the cross and the stone.

The Tara Protectum gave this warning . . .
As men are weak,
Life eternal is all they seek.
The powers may be taken once, perhaps twice.
But never, ever, thrice.
For upon the time of the third.
Man shall not speak a single word.

No sound shall be heard, made by man,
Nor fox or even singing bird.
Silence and darkness will descend,
It shall be the final end . . .

Chapter 1

LILA

Piercing the morning quiet, I heard a noise, louder than any I'd ever heard. Greater than the most tempestuous storm. The sky shook and every tree in the wood shuddered. The ground beneath my feet vibrated enough to cause me to lose footing and I fell to the ground. Then all was quiet again. What had happened? Looking around, I saw nothing appeared to change. But there was no sound, nothing, not the rustling of leaves nor the song of birds. Why?

Within the silence I heard a sound not unlike the clashing of swords. Metal against metal, and very faintly, a soft cry of pain. I followed the cries until I came upon a metal trap with its jaws clasped around the leg of a fox.

I knew I owed my first allegiance to the Cathedral, but I could not ignore an animal in pain. Though I'd been ordered to never leave the sanctuary untended, it was only a short way away.

Nothing had happened within the bower in the years I held the Position of Sentinel, why would today be an exception? Surely, they would wish me to aid an animal in distress?

REYNARD (fox)

All the times I've roamed this glen, how does it happen today, I find a trap where none had been before? This did not happen merely by chance. Someone or something is determined to make me suffer further, for a bygone transgression.

Through my pain, I saw her approach. She was small of stature, but had a presence that spoke of strength. As she knelt over me I could sense her compassion. Within her hand she held a branch, which she used to pry open the jaws of the trap.

I did not have the strength to move my leg. I'd been held so long I was unable to lift it. But she gently extracted my limb from the grasping jaws. Did I dare tell her I once held her duties? Should I warn her that merely by saving my life she may have lost her own? I think I have to risk telling her what she needs to know.

Not certain if she could understand me, I concentrated and used my mind to communicate.

Miss I am deeply gratified you rescued me, but we must return to the Cathedral at once. Though the pain was stealing my reason, I had to protect her.

Her eyes grew wide, and her mouth fell open as she struggled with the strange occurrence she just experienced. She stood and took me up in her arms and tried to speak.

"But . . . but you're a fox. How is it I understand you?"

I knew she was now the sentinel. The green stole embroidered with gold thread was proof of her office.

I was not always a fox. Like you, I was a Sentential. I will explain more once we return to the Cathedral. We cannot afford to delay.

A look of pure horror contorted her features. She grasped me tightly in the crook of her right arm and grabbed her long robe up to her knees with her left. I was held more tightly than was necessary, but I understood why she did so. It was clear she remembered her mission.

As we approached the bower, she slowed her steps.

"No, no," she cried.

"I was not gone for more than a moment. How could this have happened?" The soft calming presence within the bower had somehow been eradicated. What once had been a haven was now a dark and mysterious glade. She held me tighter and ventured further.

Her soft grey robe was tinged with my blood. Even the tips of her stole, the symbol of her office, was streaked with my life fluid.

I barked sharply, as she was squeezing the life from me. *Miss, we have to determine what has been broken, and what has been stolen.*

She released, setting me on the ground. The fur on my back raised and I grew wary. The woman searched furtively about the bower. She, too, appeared cautious. Every instinct I possessed told me more was wrong than what I could see.

Looking around, I noted little was amiss, but the feeling within the cathedral was somehow off. I remembered well the comfort just being within the leafy bower afforded. This was gone. It was as if something was blocking the sun. No rays penetrated the canopy and a chill wind swept through.

I could not stand on my leg and supporting my body on the remaining three was tiring me greatly. I barked, and she looked down on me. My paw was still bleeding. She removed her stole and tore it into strips.

She knelt beside me and again took me up in her arms. Gently she carried me to what apparently was her bed, far finer than I'd ever had while in service here. I said a silent prayer that the punishments were also less harsh. She was but a young lass and should not suffer for caring for me. Leaving me for moments only, she returned from the sacristy with a basin of tepid water. With one strip of the cloth, she cleansed my wound. Once the injury was fully revealed, it was clearly not as bad as my pain would indicate.

"There," she said.

"Now what is your name? I'm Lila."

I'm known as Reynard. I recognize your station as I, too once was sentinel.

I wanted to tell her all, but my head throbbed with the pain in my paw. The blood was slowing to a mere trickle, but still I could feel the sharp clamp of the trap.

"You were a sentinel? Here? How is it a fox is a sentinel? I had extensive training for this position."

My dear Lila, you are yet young and clearly a better choice for the Cathedral than I. I pray for the good of mankind you will remain steadfast. Something is amiss here, though no damage is yet apparent. Perhaps you were far luckier than I. I lost my station and my human form through my failure to do my diligence in protecting the cross and the sanctuary.

"But the cross is so heavy how could one person steal it? Why would anyone want to?"

I believe it has powers that exceed the strengths of mortal man. You were not gone long enough for the cross and stone to be taken. Perhaps you are saved.

"What do you mean, Reynard, *saved*?"

You are still a human woman. My transgression was far greater than yours. You sought only to aid another. We'd not yet entered the main hall of the Cathedral, nor had we seen the cross. Once my wounds were cleaned and bound, she carried me into the hall. I was certain no one could have taken the cross in the short time she was tending me. How wrong I was. The giant emerald that graced the center of the massive cross was pried from its mounting.

Lila cried out in despair, "It's damaged. I too have failed in my duties. How can this be righted?"

NATHAIRA

How foolish these simpletons be. My strength, speed, and power cannot be matched by any puny being such as these. 'Twas far more difficult to steal from him, and even more tedious taking it from the first. I had to use physical strength and mortal men to acquire the cross from them. This method is far superior. How glad am I that I have the power?

Would that it might be that my new strengths will aid me in retaining the green stone this third, final time. It shall be mine for all time.

I well remember the joy I felt cheating the first foolish Sentinel. This simpleton was felled by a soft brush of sooty lashes. Not struck against his back, the lashes that framed my eyes. I suppose since the man was probably celibate he was an easy mark. He followed me around like a puppy, doing whatever I asked no matter how senseless the request.

Though it was ten long years ago, I remember as if it happened only a moment past.

I was only fifteen but had already created a persona of a worldly woman. Gifted with a body designed for sin I readily engaged in pursuits not usually socially accepted for a girl of my age. I cared not what others thought of me only of what I could acquire that I desired.

I wanted power and wealth and would do anything to acquire them. Fortunately, I was as clever as I was comely. To turn a man to my whim was not a difficult process.

I came upon him as he emerged from a leafy bower deep in the forest. He was mumbling to himself, the same phrase over and over. *"Because of this cross you shall live forever, because of this cross you shall live forever."* He shuffled through the wood, unmindful of his direction.

To be immortal, to live forever. What a boon. If I lived forever I could acquire everything I ever desired. I must have this cross he speaks of. As I stood directly in his path, he walked straight into me. He dropped whatever he was holding and looked up at me.

"I'm sorry, I was not watching where I was going. Please forgive me. You are not harmed, are you?"

I turned my head coquettishly, smiled, and replied, "No, not harmed, only surprised. I have been in this wood many times and have never before seen another person."

"Our church is new and few venture here. This bower is the home to the first church."

He pointed behind him and I noted the overhanging branches formed an arch with a long corridor. Reaching down he picked up a small chain with numerous beads upon it. It was what he had dropped. It was now covered with dirt.

"Here, let me clean that for you. It was my fault you dropped it." I shook the talisman and wiped away the remaining earth with the sleeve of my robe.

He looked up at me, and in his eyes, all I could see was unrequited love. Here was a man so hungry for affection, he could easily turn his back on what was his most sacred duty. Gently I placed the cleaned string of beads in the palm of his hand. He looked intently at his palm as if he could not understand what had transpired and could not explain his feelings in relation to my touch. I could tell he was greatly moved, as tears formed in his eyes. Why he was so affected was a puzzle to me. It was simply a touch. Perhaps I have greater power than I realize. At least over a man who has known no physical attraction. I had many suitors, each scrambling to serve my every command. I would need them all, as the moving the massive cross is no small matter.

I placed my arm about his shoulders and drew his body tightly to mine. His cheeks flushed and he looked only at the ground. Slowly and carefully I led him away from his church. Away from his duty. Day was nearly at a close as I guided him into a nearby inn. I plied him with drink and knew nature would take its course. The Druid was handsome and many wenches were eager to share his beauty. Quietly I slipped away, confident the women would introduce him to carnal desires he knew nothing of.

AMADEAUS

My failures are all too familiar to me. When that succubus approached me, I should have been able to recognize the evil she bore. But, I was an untried youth. I thought myself immune to the wiles of seduction, that my calling would cause me to rise above such distractions. Foolish, foolish man, how easily we delude ourselves.

She was beautiful beyond compare. No woman in the entire world was her equal. The fine hair on the back of my neck stood on end when I first caught sight of her. I should have taken it as warning, but desire dismissed caution. Her eyes were a soft amber, her hair was as dark as night, and just as dangerous.

I was surrounded by women, fat ones, skinny ones, tall ones, short ones. And all fascinated me. They would lean over my table displaying their cleavage, a clear invitation to seduction. One in particular, similar in appearance to the one who brought me here, lavished me with attention and drink. I'd never before tasted sweet honeyed mead and found I enjoyed it very much. Perhaps too much, as now reason fled from my mind and what happened next is not clear.

When I finally regained my wits an entire night had passed. I had been placed upon a very soft mattress upon which were smooth soft sheets, the like of which I had never before felt. Perhaps I had not my senses returned. What if this was but a dream? I had little time to ponder my situation as suddenly the room was filled with women, each more enticing than the last. Perhaps I died and was in heaven. Though this was a far cry from what I expected of heaven, it was extremely pleasant, but not as pure as I thought heaven to be. The women fawned over me causing my body to respond in manners heretofore unknown to me. I was swept up into a passion and my desire for the women was insatiable.

Once I had dallied with each of them, I left the inn in search of other women. So I wandered for many weeks, following only my desires.

I'd been traveling mindlessly for going on a month. I stopped to rest near a village and noted there was some sort of celebration taking place. People dressed in their best finery, all sorts of entertainment, and food of every description loaded each table set upon the lawn. I slipped into a group who were watching a juggler and followed them as they moved to take part of the food. I was very hungry as I'd eaten little more than berries and nuts for weeks. No one seemed to take notice of me, so I assumed this was not a private feast.

One very beautiful woman seemed to be directing the festivities. She was dressed like a princess. Listening carefully to the crowds, I learned she was the new wife of King Arthur, one Guinevere of Cameliard. So she was, in fact, a queen.

Not behaving in a manner befitting a queen she mingled with the crowd, tossing flirtatious glances to every man in her path, regardless of his station. I noted the king did not appear to be amused. He glowered at any man who returned her glances. Within moments, the crowd grew silent. The king rose, his armor clanking against the massive wooden chair that was his throne. Barely containing his ire, he called out, "Guinevere, attend me at once."

The beautiful queen raised her head, glared at the regent, turned away, and walked to the nearby wood.

I thought it my duty to inform the young queen, kings do not like being ignored. Thus, I followed her, to console and advise her. She had not ventured deeply into the wood and I easily found her sitting at the edge of a small pond. Dipping her fingers in the water, she stared at the surface and the trails her finger had made. She was completely absorbed in the mindless activity and did not hear my approach.

"Excuse me, my lady, would you accept some advice from a Druid who knows what it is to ignore rules?"

Slowly she lifted her lashes and stared at me. Smiling broadly, she bid me sit beside her. Happily, I complied. Her scent wafted toward me on a gentle summer breeze. I was at once enchanted, and reason fled my mind. She was intoxicating. I had to possess this wondrous creature. To make her mine. Lust ruled my thoughts. Slowly I put my arm about her shoulders. She should have brushed me away as a proper married woman, but she did not. Leaning into my embrace, she sighed and snuggled closer to me. She lifted her head from my chest and presented her lips to me. I could not, as I should have, ignore her invitation.

I embraced her and lowered my lips to hers. Quickly I realized what I was doing and stopped. Her husband was the king. She looked up and said, "I care not what my husband does, he pays little mind to me."

"But, my Queen, you have been married only a short time. Surely he pays attention to you."

"It has been but seven months, but seven months with Arthur is like seven years in purgatory."

"That cannot be so."

"Ah, but it is. Come, my little Druid, make my life the heaven it should be. I will love you with all of my heart and soul."

Her tale was so intriguing, I could not, would not, resist. I gave her my heart. In my mind, I gave it for all time. However, the fates had other plans. We wandered throughout the summer, taking our pleasure where we might.

As sure as fall follows summer, our time came to an abrupt end. In a broad meadow at the edge of the Scottish border, horses came thundering across the grass. Approximately a hundred horsemen came upon us.

The leader called for his men to halt, removed his headpiece, and demanded, "My Queen, you are to return to King Arthur at once. He's stood your foolishness long enough. It is time you realized you are a queen and must perform the duties of that office."

I knew she would tell him she loved me and would remain with me for all time. That Arthur would have to select another to share his throne.

But she did not. Meekly she said, "I know, it is time. Come, take me to Arthur."

She did not even glance back at me as she sat upon the white palfrey they provided for her and rode away. Out of my life forever.

I felt as if my heart had been ripped from my chest by a dragon claw, and the pain swarmed over me as blood from a mortal wound.

REYNARD

I don't know why I felt I should have compassion for the man who stole the heart of our queen. King Arthur was beside himself with grief. Wondering if she were hurt or killed, or that she simply no longer wished to be queen.

He'd sent out scores of men searching for her. I sent a message to the King when we found her. He bid me follow her and to not allow her to know she was being watched. The King, a wise man, allowed her a few days to adventure as he was certain this was the reason she fled. She was young and unused to responsibility. But he could wait no longer. He charged me with finding and returning her. I knew little of her escape, only that it was believed she headed to Arthur's church, that he had ordered constructed in her honor. A self-centered lass, she was enchanted that something no matter how primitive, was to be built to respect her faith. Arthur had long embraced the olde ways. His most trusted advisor Merlin was a Druid. But he chose to honor his queen. After the third day, I approached her.

"Your Highness, you must return to Camelot." I extended my hand to assist her to mount behind me. She took it, but clearly it was a reluctant move. Feeling that she was safely upon the horse, I urged the animal forward. We'd gone only a matter of feet, when I felt her push against my back and throw herself off. As it had rained the previous evening, she landed in the mud. She stood and brushed at her skirts, but the wet muck clung tenaciously. Were the anger in her eyes, fire, I would have been consumed like dry straw. She stamped her feet, clenched her fists, and screamed, like a toddler in a tantrum. Though I did not wish to have her in front of me, I thought it best to assure her safety. Then she determined to use a different tact. Flashing her eyes at me over her shoulder, she wiggled against me.

"Your Highness, please be still."

"Why? Don't you like the feel of me against you?"

"It is not proper my Queen."

"Oh poo on proper. You sound like Arthur. You must do this, you must do that. Must, must. I hate that word. Come on admit it, you like me, don't you?" she asked coquettishly.

I stopped the horse and called my second in command to my side. "Officer Neeley, take this woman, bind her hands, and put her on your mount."

The anger in her eyes flared again, "How dare you treat me like a common criminal? I will see that you lose your precious position, and I am certain the king will banish you."

I knew she was a soft spot in Arthur's heart, but I was equally confident he would not question his most loyal man. Thus, I ignored her taunts.

Neeley was not happy I'd chosen him as the Queen's guardian. He muttered under his breath, "Pretty little manipulator." She heard him and screeched at him something unintelligible.

I turned her to face me and ordered her to be quiet. "Whilst I am loath to do so, I will gag you."

"You wouldn't dare?" she replied, shocked she'd not enticed me.

I answer only to Arthur, not an immature child.

"Then cease your prattle. I'll hear no further outbursts from you. Understand? These woods are not be the safest part of our journey. You will not endanger my troops."

She spoke not another word, but I could tell she was plotting what to relate to Arthur about her unjust treatment.

In a matter of hours we arrived at Camelot's gates. Guinevere spoke softly. "Sir, would you please remove my restraints? I do not wish my subjects to see me in this fashion."

"Neeley, remove her bindings." As he did so, I noted an evil glint in her eyes. She rubbed her wrists and drew herself to her full height.

Arthur rode out to greet us. The very moment she saw him, her shoulders slumped, and she began to weep, her haughty manner dropped. She whined, "Arthur, you cannot believe how these rogues have treated me. They bound me like a common thief. Oh, my King, I am so glad to be home."

"Reynard, what is the meaning of this? How dare you treat my wife in such a manner?"

"Your Highness, I assure you she was restrained for her own safety. She deliberately threw herself from my horse and landed in the mud.

Sire, you can see for yourself the state of her attire. I dared not risk her further harm."

Arthur smiled briefly, and shook his head. I can see he is questioning his choice of a queen. The king ordered her off the horse. "Guinevere, you are confined to your quarters until, I determine what action should be taken."

She stamped her feet and flounced up the stairs to her rooms.

Personally, I felt the young woman was too flighty and not fit to be queen. Her constant flirtations with every male who caught her eye, were very unseemly for a regent. I was certain the poor cleric was enchanted by the woman and deserved consideration not chastisement. I knew him from the meeting where the king set up the council for building the church. This Druid was set up as the first sentinel. Arthur would be displeased that the man had failed in his duty and far more than displeased, that he'd absconded with the queen. Yet the poor fool was but a pawn in Guinevere's game.

"Reynard, I fail to see that you or your men have done anything unseemly, but I now have a mission for you. The Druid must tell me his part of this sordid tale. You are to find him and return him to me."

"As you wish, Sire. May we eat and clean up afore we set out?"

"Of course, of course. You may also need more supplies, as I have no idea where this man might be."

Arthur was a fine ruler the like of which had never before been seen in England. Even many Scots revered the man.

After a hearty meal, we set out to find Amadeaus. The skies were clear and showed no sign of rain. He should be easy to track once we found someone who had seen the man. I knew he would not have wandered far from the church, once he realized he'd been used by the woman. Truly, it would be his only refuge.

We came upon him sitting on a rock near a stream, just outside the Green Cathedral. His feet were in the water but he'd not bothered to remove his sandals. He looked up and down the length of the stream and then shook his head.

I signaled for my men to halt, even the clinking of the harnesses and stamping of horses hooves, had not moved the man. He appeared to be in some type of trance. I then noticed his shoulders were shaking. The poor man was sobbing like a child. I approached the Druid and did my best to console the man. What had transpired was not the fault of the cleric. He was an innocent. He looked up at me, his tormented soul exposed. I led him to my horse and bid him mount.

As the cathedral was only a short distance from the palace we arrived before the sun set. Amadeaus seemed to be emerging from his trance like state. When we reached the gates, the sun was fully set and many lights graced Camelot. Stable boys came and cared for our mount. We went immediately to the council room, where the king was perusing some documents spread out on the round table.

Arthur bid the Druid approach. "Amadeaus, you have greatly disappointed me. I thought to bring cooperation between the olde ways and the new. Your open mindedness convinced me I had chosen correctly. Apparently, I had not.

Arthur's response was a surprise to me. "Sir Reynard, you have served me well and I trust you above other men. Return to the church. You will now take over the position the Druid failed to serve."

"But Sire, I am a knight, not a churchman. How can I perform the duties of a priest? Cannot the Druid resume his post once he's seen the error of his ways?"

"It is precisely your skill as a knight that is required. You are far more worldly than the Druid. You shall not be as easily enticed, as was the cleric. It is your mission to preserve and protect the church. Have the fool man instruct you as to what other services you are to perform. You will be the Sentinel."

NATHAIRA

Why do I always have to deal with incompetents? They are smart enough to revere me, you'd think they could follow simple orders as easily as they follow their lust.

"You there, brace that cross piece or the entire thing will fall on you."

"My name is Luke, Mistress."

"Yes, Luke, you will take greater care. It is your responsibility and I expect you to perform as I have directed." I really don't care what his name is, as long as he does as he is told. As each of them vies for my attention, they are not minding the task at hand.

Perhaps I should select one to favor and place him in charge of the others?

"Luke, I know I can depend on you. I am placing you in charge of this mission. Those who perform the best for you will be amply rewarded. It goes without saying, you too will be compensated, if the job is completed successfully. Do you understand me?"

"I do, Mistress. You will be well pleased. I shall see all is done in the manner you require."

There is no doubt Luke will get the job done properly, but dealing with him after the cross is in my custody, will be another cross for me to bear. I recognize all too well the signs of greed. He will want a greater portion than I feel is his due.

Rather than have to watch his every move I drew away from the site.

Should there be a problem, I will be well away from any punishment.

I was just out of sight of the church when I heard the thundering of hooves, many hooves. Not a passing stranger, but a troop of horsemen. Luke ordered his men to flee. They did so leaving the cross still in place. I had failed. It may be some time before another opportune moment occurs.

I crept back hiding in the brush to see what actually had happened. Men were dismantling my scaffolding tearing down the braces and pulleys. They were destroying valuable equipment. Equipment, for which I'd paid dearly. One very striking man was issuing orders.

"All this must be destroyed. No one shall ever use this stuff to deface this church or any other. See it is all burned," he directed. Atop his dark stallion he cut a dashing figure.

How dare he? I'd worked months to acquire this equipment and even longer to insure the fleeting loyalty of the men utilizing it. This man I shall watch closely. I'd never seen these men before but for a certainty they were the King's men. It was clear they were setting up an encampment. They would be here for a while. It would give me time to study them and determine their motives. Not appearing to be either Druids or priests, I am confident they will merely secure the cross and when they encounter little resistance, they will move on, as soldiers always do.

Perhaps this handsome leader could be seduced? Probably more difficult to entice than the cleric, but a man that comely was no stranger to women.

The man ordered his soldier to capture my men. They set out but he remained, and began to search the nearby wood. I leaned forward parting the ferns and just as he turned, he caught sight of me. His horse reared, yet he easily got the animal under control.

"Calm yourself Duncan, it's only a woman."

Only a woman? This man is as foolish as he is handsome. I am not *only* a woman, I am far more than any other woman he's encountered. I stepped into the small clearing, lowered my head ever so slightly, and then peered up at him through my eyelashes. He seemed interested but not enamored, as most men were. Something other than lust drives this man. Once I discover it, he shall be under my control, just as completely as the Druid.

REYNARD

I should have known poor Amadeaus would be easy prey for those who would deter him from his mission. She will find, I am not so easily duped. Not that Her Highness would attempt another seduction. Particularly not with me. She now knows better and I am certain Arthur will keep a tighter rein on her, lest she chooses to repeat her folly.

I do not understand how Amadeaus failed to treat the Queen with respect. Her feminine wiles must be very enticing. Hopefully Arthur will be temperate in his punishment. The poor Druid will never forgive himself, but the King should.

Knowing the church was secure, I decided to return to the cathedral at a leisurely trot. However the massive stallion didn't wish to travel at such a pace, he wanted to run. He pulled against the bridle, until I gave him his head. His hooves thundered against the hard-packed dirt, throwing up divots of earth. He and I ran many races and always emerged the victors. When funds were short, before I was in Arthur's service, I survived quite well on our winnings. I loved the rush of the wind against my face as much as Duncan did. I actually won the animal on a wager. I'd won and lost many fortunes before I won Duncan. Now, I never lost. He was a Brabant Draft horse. Possessing deceptive speed and heavy legs, Duncan led many a fool to believe he could be easily beaten. Somewhat short, his power made up for his size. He is my most prized possession.

However, in Arthur's forces there is little opportunity to wager. The King frowned upon gambling. He believed it led to other vices, that could cripple an army. I suppose one could lose sight of a goal if the stakes were high and the gambler greedy. My wagers were merely for the thrill of the win not the monetary gain. However, there is a fine line between the exhilaration of the contest and the desire for the coin.

Leaning over I patted Duncan's neck and urged him to a slower gait. He is an exquisite piece of horseflesh and I had no desire to lose him. I lead him to a stream and allowed him to drink. When his thirst was satisfied, I removed my grooming tools from my pack and began to brush down his sleek dappled coat.

He arched his back against the brush as he reveled in my ministrations. His mane was long and luxurious, and I combed it out until it shown like a dark river on a moonlight night. I took great pride in Duncan. My possessions were few and most of my worth was negligible, but the horse was beyond price.

Fortunately being in Arthur's service I received a steady wage and was not required to wager to survive.

The green church had more than just the church proper. The housing for the sentinel, a tidy stable and a storage shed for provisions, were on the grounds. I led Duncan into the warm barn. He snorted, stamped his hooves and walked into the largest stall. Duncan was as aristocratic as a horse could possibly be. He thought himself to be royalty and expected to be treated as such.

I'd left Neeley in charge and was certain he and his men would safeguard the cross. Going to the encampment they set up just outside of the church grounds to confer with him, I found only a limited number of guards remaining.

"Officer Neeley, why are there so few men here? Are there sufficient men to safeguard the cross? In view of the severity of the situation, I would think you would desire to have a larger force at your disposal."

"Sir, I understand your concern, but I've allowed some men to attend a large racing match at a nearby faire ground. I've reserved the finest men to guard the Cathedral. Trust me Sir, I realize what is at stake. Neither would I risk your wrath or that of the King. All is secure I assure you."

"My ears perked up at his mention of the racing match. It's been a long time since Duncan and I raced and I felt the need as eagerly as my horse. Did I dare to take the time to enjoy an afternoon's wagering? Neely would guard the church with as much diligence as I.

And, I would not be countermanding Arthur's directive. I swear Duncan could smell the race ground as he strained against the bit. Holding him in check was no easy task. A draft horse is a very powerful animal, but I did not want him to reveal his strength to those we would compete against.

Dismounting I approached the wagering table and bet on myself. The counter looked at me with a raised eyebrow.

"Pretty confident, aren't ye? I feel it my duty to inform you, should ye race this day ye are against the most successful animal in these competitions. And Black Duff has never lost since he acquired Kansbar."

"Kansbar, I don't believe I've ever heard of him. I do however, believe I can beat him."

"As ye wish, lad, best luck."

Kansbar was a Persian name, a group of peoples who were renowned for their skills at breeding horses. I stepped to the area where the competing horses were stationed, tying Duncan's reins to the lead line, I examined the stock I would be racing against. All were fine animals, but none that would give me pause.

As I was evaluating the competition a very tall sleek horse approached, ridden by the largest man I have ever seen. He was in full armor, though few races were run in with the contestants so burdened. His mount was near to 17 hands high, and possessed an arrogance I'd never before seen in a horse. The animal actually looked down his nose at me. His rider lifted his visor and gave me a similar glance. His armor was as dark as his mount and shone with a sheen that reflected the sunlight. His game was clearly intimidation, a game I would not play. I was confident Duncan could best his mount.

As he dismounted, I approached and extended my hand in the spirt of good sportsmanship. He looked down at it and turned away abruptly. So that's the way it is to be. Fine, I have no strong desire for the man's friendship.

Several men rode their animals to the starting line. The contestants and their horses were announced. I noted the dark knight was not among them. I had been assigned to the second race and hoped Black Duff would be as well. The first competition was completed and contestants for the second were approaching the starting line. The big man, still in full armor, was beside me. His horse stamped his feet and snorted. The horse was as good at intimidation as his master, but Duncan was unimpressed. He stood still and apparently not competitive, I knew, however, he was as eager for the race as was I.

The starter cracked a whip and the horses lurched ahead. Duncan set out slowly as if he were simply taking a leisurely stroll. Kansbar was confused and wasted valuable time looking back to see why Duncan was moving so slowly.

As the competition reached the mid-point, Duncan lowered his head and thrust himself forward, his massive hooves thundered against the earth with such a force the ground shuddered. His powerful shoulders pumping his muscular legs, threw up huge clots of ground. Kansbar had made up the ground he lost by looking back and was close at Duncan's flank. I swear I could feel his hot breath on my neck, he was so close.

It was then Duncan switched his gait and long loping strides carried him to the finish line.

I went to the wagering table to collect my winnings. Black Duff strode up beside me, saying, "You did not win fairly. That animal is not even a race horse, and I am in full armor."

"My good man, nowhere in any race I have taken part of is it stated the horse must be of racing stock, nor is a rider required to wear armor. That was your choice."

Duff was not deterred, he removed his helm and threw it on the ground. "I challenge you to another race just between the two of us, without general wagers. When I win, I will have that horse.

Chapter 2

NATHERIA

Ah, how sweet the smell of victory. Reynard has fallen into my trap even quicker than I anticipated. He won the first even though I was certain he would not. Now Duff has cornered him into a head-to-head challenge. And, to make the pot a little sweeter, I will not have to compensate the black knight, he will easily win and have the powerful animal for himself. All I need do now is keep the fool away from the Green Cathedral long enough to steal the cross. An easy task.

I directed my attention to the racecourse, where Duff was removing his armor as well as the heavy plates that covered his mount. The horse appeared nervous, stamping his feet and throwing his head side to side. Duff attempted to control the animal by pulling down on Kansbar's bridle. This was not to the horses' liking. He reared and kicked out at Duff narrowly missing the knight's head.

Reynard seemed to be enjoying Duff's situation. He leaned against Duncan and crossed his legs in a casual pose.

Duff now had his animal under control and was resetting the bit. Reynard mounted, and turned his horse to the racecourse. Slowly, he set himself at the starting line. Black Duff drew alongside and smiled.

"You haven't won yet Duff, and now you know it will never happen."

Duff replied haughtily, "Nor have you, and I have divested myself of the only handicap, within moments I shall have your horse."

The whip snapped and the combatants strained ahead, each animal giving it his all. Nothing was held back. Duncan used his sturdy legs to propel himself and Kansbar utilized his impressive stride to gain ground. It was a close race. First Duncan led, then Kansbar's gallop drew him ahead. Hooves pounding the ground throwing up dirt and dust, for a moment it was difficult to see who was winning.

But, when the dust cleared, it was Kansbar who was the victor.

REYNARD

I lost? I lost, but how? I've never lost. I cannot part with Duncan. He is the only thing in this world that gives me my reason for being. Even my worth to Arthur is based on my horse. Perhaps if I don't dismount the Duff will accept another payment.

This most likely would not be the case. Duff strolled up to me, his horses' reins in his hand. Reaching out he indicated I was to place Duncan's reins alongside of Kansbar's.

"I'm sorry, Duff, but you will have to accept another form of payment. I will not part with my horse."

We were almost at eye level even though he was standing on the ground. He shook his head and said, "I'm sorry, but the wager stands. I beat you and you will surrender your mount."

"See here, I understand I lost and I will be happy to honor the debt, but you will have to state another form of payment. My custom sword, perhaps."

I would hate to lose the sword as it was specially commissioned by Arthur for me. It was actually forged to my exact measurements. Though I did not purchase it, it was of considerable value.

"That, sir, is not acceptable. The stakes were the horses. You lost, I won. Your animal is mine. But to show you I am a fair man, I will give you three months to repurchase the animal at twice his current value."

I stammered. Duncan was a near priceless animal. How would his worth be determined?

"And, who shall determine his value? You cannot simply say the animal is worth a certain amount."

"Quite so, the animal will be appraised by a breeder of considerable renown. I am certain you will know of him. However, double the amount is what I require to relinquish Duncan."

I know there is more to this situation than is apparent to me. He has an agenda beyond acquiring my horse. As the wager was announced and there are many witnesses, I have little recourse but to do as the Black Duff demands.

I dismounted and reluctantly handed over Duncan's reins. I was certain the horse would rather remain with me, but I had no other option.

"Duncan," I said as I stoked his muzzle, "I'll get you back somehow. Never fear, we are a team. I don't know how but we shall be together again. I swear it."

He raised his head and shook off my hand. The animal was actually mad at me. *Trust me fellow, losing you was not my plan.* As Duff lead him away, he turned and there was a tear in his eye. I must get him back, no matter what it takes.

LILA

Why I am being taken from the Cathedral? I've done nothing wrong. The King's guard tells me I must go to Camelot. Is the king angry with me? I've done everything as he directed. I only left the sanctuary momentarily. I could not let the fox suffer. It is one of God's creatures after all. Surely, I cannot be blamed for the evil that attempted to steal the stone? I do not believe I could have stopped them even if I had been there. There had to be far more than one person to scale the cross and extract the gem.

"Lila, please keep up with the rest of us. It is not a long journey but the heavy fog is making it difficult. If you don't feel comfortable on your own horse, you may certainly ride with one of us."

"I fear I am not accustomed to riding as I spent most of my time in the church, studying and copying manuscripts."

"Perhaps then it might be better if you ride with me. My horse can easily accommodate two riders."

"Sir Bors, I appreciate the offer but I would not wish to overburden your mount."

"Nonsense, these animals are trained to carry a rider and a wounded man. Since you are neither wounded nor a man, I am certain your slight weight won't tax the horse overmuch."

I would much prefer to ride with someone rather than try to navigate this fog and unfamiliar ground. My mind is brimming with questions and I have no wish to try to figure out where I am going.

"If you are certain, I would prefer to accompany you on your horse. Do you know where we are going? Can you find your way in this fog?"

"Fear not, my lady, the horse well knows the way to a warm stable and fresh grain. We shall not become lost."

He pulled me up onto his horse and set me astride his lap. I was so tired. Leaning against him I quickly fell asleep. He was warm and comfortable. I felt safe.

It seemed only moments when he spoke. "My lady, we are drawing near to Camelot. It is not seemly for you to be so intimately against my chest."

My God, the man was insinuating I was attempting to seduce him. "I am sorry if I have offended your sensibilities. Rest assured, I was merely tired, I have no intentions regarding your person."

"Please, my lady, you mistake my meaning. I made the suggestion that you might right your person and perhaps smooth your gown before you meet the King and Queen. I can see you are a woman of quality and would hate for you to be taken for anything less than that."

My anger tempered. He was simply behaving as a person concerned for my reputation. Though a large and intimidating man he was kind and considerate.

"Please forgive my misunderstanding. I am not a worldly sort of woman and find it strange that sometimes people's motives are hard to ascertain."

"I fully understand. I, too, have been tested many times and often wonder if I am doing what the good Lord would wish of me."

"I truly appreciate your consideration. Can you tell me some things about the King and Queen? I never actually met them even though I work for them."

Sir Bors regaled me with tales of Camelot and how grand it was and how noble was King Arthur, but I was growing weary. I slumped back against his chest and fell asleep. It seemed I'd only drifted off when the knight shook me, saying, "We're here, my lady. Perhaps you would like some water and to brush the dust of travel from your person. We cannot be seen from the castle as yet, so you will have plenty of time."

I shook my head to clear my thoughts and took Sir Bors' hand to aid me in the dismount. When my feet touched the ground it seemed my legs would not hold me. The knight slid from his horse and caught me before I fell.

When I looked up at him, I noticed he was quite handsome. I blushed, something I've done only very rarely. The sensation both intrigued and scared me. Was I attracted to the man? A man I hardly know. Maybe he is the one. He warms my body in ways I've never felt before. He cast a knowing glance in my direction.

"I know, Lady Lila, I sense it too. We are being tested. We must resist. For me it is but another trial. For you I imagine it is the first of many challenges."

However strong my feelings for the knight and though there was a sense of connection, I knew deep within my heart that the fox was fated to be my companion. How I know this I do not understand, but I know for a certainty he is my destiny. I quickly made myself more presentable and we approached the castle.

Camelot lived up to its reputation. Every stone appeared to have been hand-selected. Each one blending into the next. The drawbridge was constructed of a white oak and the mechanism cogs and chain were crafted perfectly. Beneath, the waters of the moat were crystal clear and on the surface swam the most beautiful swans, both black and white. As we entered the bailey I noted not only was there ample area for the many crafts that served the people, there were all about the perimeter, splendid gardens.

Once we were inside the gate Sir Bors helped me dismount, a groomsman approached took our mounts and I was left to stare in awe at the beauty that surrounded me. From what appeared to be the doors to the castle proper a group of young women approached. At the head of the ladies was a very beautiful blond woman. I wondered if she was the fabled Guinevere. I hoped I was presentable. Straightening my collar, I felt my cross was missing. It had been my mother's and it was all I had left of her. A strange sensation overtook me and a tear slipped down my cheek. I knew it would not be judicious to weep as I met the Queen, so I swallowed my heartache and wiped away the tear. Extending her hand the lady introduced herself.

"Good day to you, Lady Lila, I am the queen."

I was going to extend my hand when I noticed Sir Bors shake his head slightly and bow, so subtlety, it wasn't obvious to anyone save me. I bowed, deeply and addressed the regent.

"Good day to you, Your Highness. Your home is quite beautiful."

She tossed back her blond curls over her shoulder and said," I suppose it is. Come, ladies, Lila follow us to your quarters."

The girls tagged along closely like ducklings following their mother. The Queen lifted her chin and strode regally through the open courtyard up to the door from whence she came.

I had to practically run to keep up, they moved so swiftly through a myriad of corridors. I hoped I would be able to find my way out if I were not lead. Suddenly, Guinevere stopped. Two of the ladies came around and opened the double doors in front of her.

The room was more grand than any I had ever seen. Rich tapestries covered gilded walls, sumptuous carpets were beneath our feet, and there were windows. Such glorious windows, covered with stained glass. This could not be my quarters.

"Your Highness, is this were I am to stay?"

"Oh, don't be silly you foolish girl. You will sleep with the ladies across the hallway. Now go, shoo all of you." We were summarily dismissed. The group moved to a room opposite the queen's.

One stayed behind the group. She addressed me, saying, "Lady Lila, fear not, I will aid you. You have met the queen and her little bees. I've been here the longest and find I am no longer enamored of the trappings of court. I will show you what you need to know."

"What is your name, Mistress?"

"I am known as Lady Clare, I've been with her highness since we were girls. I used to be her chief counsel, but she no longer relies on me for advice."

"And why is that, my lady?" I knew instinctively, this woman was the right one to cultivate as a friend. She was privy to the inner workings of the castle and its courtiers. Information I might very well need.

"You seem a bit naïve, Lady Lila. Please keep our conversations between us and no one else. You never know who might be listening and may distort the conversation to vicious gossip." Her voice caught, stifling her trepidation. I am certain she was recalling a previous uncomfortable situation.

Lady Clare was now in tears. I placed my arm about her shoulders and hugged her. The loss of a life-long friend is difficult to bear. It was clear she loved the Queen and feared the change in her childhood friend might end in disaster.

Noticing the other ladies were moving toward us, she quickly dried her tears and took my elbow. She led me to an alcove off the main room. It was small, just enough room for two sleeping pallets and two chairs. There was a small brazier that give off enough heat to make the room cozy.

"You will stay with me. The others are often quite silly and I find this small haven saves my sanity."

"Tis quite homey, I thank you for sharing it with me. Do you perhaps know why I am here?"

"You are the lady from Arthur's newest church, are you not?"

"I am. At least I was. Someone tried to steal the stone while I was momentarily away. I'm told the King wants to see me. I don't know if I'm to be punished or allowed to return to my duties."

"Arthur is quite the stickler about duty. Why did you leave?"

"I heard cries of pain. They were quite close, so I reasoned I could help. I was gone only moments to free the fox from the jaws of the trap."

"Surely you would not be punished for assisting a creature in pain? Did the animal flee once it was free?"

"It did, but not before I felt a strong connection to the animal. Please tell no one. They will think I'm daft. He spoke to me."

Her eyes grew wide. "He spoke to you?" It was clear she found my revelation astounding. She clasped her hands together and hid them in the folds of her skirt. She bid me sit on her narrow bed. I, too, was overwhelmed by the event.

Now the tears were forming in my eyes.

"Yes, he truly did. Not words like between you and me, but speech in my mind. I know he is to be an important part of my life."

Lady Clare looked puzzled, she opened her mouth to speak, then apparently thought better of it. She placed her index finger across her lips, shook her head, and said, "Lady Lila, I will share this with no one and I think you should do the same. Wagging tongues often lead to slit throats."

I grasped my own throat, "Whatever do you mean? Surely some might say I was insane, but no one would kill me for it. Would they?"

"They might, my lady." I would be wise to defer to her wisdom. She was unlike the other ladies. More worldly, more polished and certainly more wise.

LADY CLARE

The Queen seemed particularly haughty this day. No doubt concerned by the beauty of Lady Lila.

"Lady Clare, did you see how close little Lady Lila was to Sir Bors?"

Ah, my dear friend, you are so easily bored. Seeking attention from your male of the moment.

The Queen abused her power simply for amusement. Her eyes snapped with rage. She pointed to one of her ladies. "You, find Sir Bors and bring him to me at once." She turned briskly.

"I want to know just how close those two became on their journey. They seemed to me to be rather intimate."

"But Gwen, why do you care? She's an innocent young girl. Arthur chose her for his church. I'm certain she has no designs on the knight."

"Well, I'm not convinced."

She was becoming absurd. Arms crossed, she paced from one end of the solar to the other, turning so sharp that her skirts snapped and her slippers hissed against the marble tile. "Bess, I forbid you to use my first name. You will always refer to me as Your Highness."

Before her tirade went further, there was a knock on the door. "Enter," she shouted. In the casement stood Sir Bors, still wearing his armor. So large he blocked the sun through the window.

"You asked to see me, Your Highness?"

Gwen looked all about the room in apparent confusion.

Was she realizing how foolish was her request or was she fearful tales of her behavior would reach the ear of the king?

Finally she gathered her senses and spoke to the knight.

"Yes, Sir Bors, I did. I did wish to speak with you. Come closer."

The knight advanced and at once Guinevere's eyes grew wide as she stared at the man. She then grew contemplative, and her eyes narrowed to mere slits, filled with pure jealousy.

"What is that hanging from your mail? It does not appear to be something a man of your stature would wear on his shoulder, no less."

The armored man looked to one shoulder then the other. He reached down and extracted a cross and chain from one of the links of his mail. "Tis not mine, Your Highness, must have come from the lass I was instructed to bring to Arthur."

"And how well acquainted are you with Lady Lila? I saw only your horse. How did the lady transport?"

"Her mount was frightening to a lass who had never before ridden, so I took her upon my mount."

"I see and did you perhaps do more with the lady than bring her to Camelot?"

The knight was indignant. "Majesty, I would never comprise a woman." I could not see how Gwen would accuse a knight of Arthur's Round Table. Arthur knew the woman was an innocent and he placed her in the charge of the finest of his knights.

I had to speak, "Your Highness, you simply cannot impugn this knight's good name." I implored, to no avail. She would not see reason.

"Bess, leave me. In fact, I have had enough of you. Pack your things at once. You will leave Camelot. Now go!"

AMADEAUS

I am the most fortunate of men. Even though I failed, the king has allowed me to return to my post, though not in the same capacity. The woods that were once so familiar to me, seem strange and uncharted. I do not recall the journey from Camelot to the church being so vast and dark. Perhaps I have taken a wrong turn somewhere? It seems the trip is endless.

Then I heard a twig snap and I turned swiftly around. Deep in the underbrush were a pair of eyes, the scant patches of sunlight reflected from them. I sat down and did not move. Whoever or whatever was hidden, began to emerge from the foliage. Not daring to move toward the creature I slowly extracted a crust of bread from my foodstuffs.

It was a fox of average size, its coat was a deep russet, and through its hide, ribs protruded. It salivated once it saw the bread, drool dripping from its mouth. The animal was clearly undernourished. In fact, the poor thing was starved. Why I wondered? The forest is full of rodents, insects, and many other things foxes regard as food. Did this one not know how to forage for itself?

As I extended the bread, the animal walked warily toward me. Daintily it took the crust from my hand. Strangely, the fox did not seem to fear me. After he consumed his meager meal, he sat back on his haunches and began to groom himself.

"Friend fox, what might be your name be?" Now, I heard not a word, but inside my head was the answer to my question.

Reynard, good Sir, what is yours?

How can this be? Have I lost my mind, as well as my way? Reynard? Is that not the name of one of Arthur's knights?" It is, I was once that very same man.

This is astounding, how can an animal have once been a man? Am I hallucinating? Or is this the Lord's punishment for failing to do my duty?

Neither, friend friar. What has happened, I am certain is part of a grand design.

"But, I did not speak aloud, how did you know what I was thinking?"

All animals speak to one another like this. Saving sound only for danger or new source of food. Not all animals can converse with man as I do, but I think it is because I was once a man.

"Whatever did you do that you lost your humanity?" This was a revelation. My punishment was far less harsh than the solider endured. *I failed in my duty to King Arthur and the Green Cathedral.* My eyes grew wide and I started to cry. I stumbled and walked backward to sit upon a large rock. The fox followed and sat beside me on the ground.

"On my soul, I thought I was the only one who failed in such a manner. Arthur himself chose me to be the Sentinel. A significant honor, and one I was undeserving of. I allowed myself to be lured and enraptured by the fairer sex. I was a slave to my desires. Until they all left me, alone and broken."

Well, at least you were left a man. I lost all my humanity, my horse, my station and Arthur's trust.

"Well," I replied, "There is nothing we can do about it now."

Not so, my friend, we can find the church and protect it until Arthur sends reinforcements.

"But how? Nothing seems as it was. I do not recognize anything around me."

Nor do I, but we can rely on my sense of smell. At least there is that. I have a far stronger method of detecting, than simply relying on my sight.

I could sense both trepidation, and determination in the fox's demeanor. This tiny fox would not be deterred no matter the difficulty of the task. Though the failure weighed heavy on my mind, I could do no less than Reynard. Together, we would save Arthur's Green Cathedral.

Chapter 3

REYNARD

It seemed we wandered for months, though I am certain it was only was only weeks. We were both tired, and, as we ate little on our journey, hungry to the bone as well. Raising my snout to the oncoming wind, I caught the scent of human food. Not fresh, but at this point I would welcome moldy cheese.

Amedeaus, I've caught the scent of food and a faint stench of a wicked mist.

"Who do you think it might be? How do you detect a mist?"

I searched my mind and could not come up with an answer, but I knew it was evil for it smelled like brimstone.

At once, the heavens opened. The rain fell in heavy torrents. My fur clung to my skin and the cold water chilled me to the bone. I could see the stinking mist forming a ball. It rolled and I quickly followed its path. The mist was shrinking into a reptilian entity, and completely slithered beneath a mass of tangled vines that blocked further exploration.

I'd left the poor Druid as I raced to determine where the mist was going. I could hear him behind me as he strained to breathe. Turning back, I went to his side as he sat on a large rock trying to catch his wind.

I think I've found the church, but our way is blocked with a heavy overgrowth of twisted vines. Do you have anything that would cut through them?

The man looked down at me, his eyes filled with tears. "I've nothing. Priests do not carry weapons. Are you certain the church lays on the other side?"

I understood his guilt, but crying was not going to rectify the situation. *Get back on track, man, we have a job to do. Do you still have your eating knife? Did you ever have to dig for food when you were the sentinel?* I was growing impatient with his all-consuming grief. I'd done far worse, but I'd be damned if it would keep me from my duty to Arthur.

Apparently the Druid sensed my discontent as he quickly reached into his cloak and extracted a small knife. He then quickly left. Where did he go and why? My questions were answered in a moment, as he reappeared carrying a sharp spade.

"It is what I used to bury fallen comrades. Will it serve our needs? I kept it in yon shed," he said, pointing to a small, dilapidated outbuilding.

It will, once I can cut through the vines, but it is not going to be an easy task. Please place the knife in my mouth and I will cut what I can, until there is enough room for you to enter.

Turning my head from side to side, I slashed at the vines creating a small opening for myself. Once though through the vines, they seemed to wither before my eyes. Yet the mist still prevailed. It hovered just above the ground, leaving only enough clear air near the ground that I might breathe. What light filtered through the canopy, over the cross revealed the stone was still in place. I started back when I noticed Amadeaus, hacking at the fallen vines and attempting to completely clear the entrance.

Stop! I shouted, but he was too intent on his task and paid me no heed. Soon he'd cleared enough that he might enter the church. Again I cried out, *Amadeaus, stop, the mist is not fit to breathe.* I was too late. Where he stood, the mist covered his head and torso. He wavered, then fell in a heap on the hard ground. I had to get him to clear air or to somehow clear away this mist. As it was now concentrated around the cleric, the stench intensified. It smelled like eggs broken and left in the sun. I had no idea of the origin of the foul-smelling fog, but I hoped it would remain where it was if I were able to drag the Druid to clear air. I grabbed his hood in my teeth and pulled. At the pace I am able to move him, I will be at this task all night. He seemed to rouse and sat up. Once his head was again within the mist, he fell back onto the ground. I stepped on his chest and held him down when he was again able to breathe.

Stay down. As long as you are beneath the fog, you will be able to breathe, once you put your head in the evil cloud you will pass out.

"All right, sir knight, I'll stay down. Groveling should be my position anyway. Surely this is my punishment, however I wonder if it is from God, the work of the Devil's minion or perhaps the haughty Guinevere is to blame."

Why would you suspect the queen?

"*Twas she who let me astray. How did she do so?*"

"Well, in truth, a very beautiful woman lured me from the church. She was more beautiful than any woman I have ever seen. Her beauty was mesmerizing. I followed her like a love-sick calf."

Are you speaking of the Queen or this beauteous woman? For whom did you abandon your post?

"Well the beauty led me to an ale house, but 'twas Lady Guinevere who drew me into debauchery."

Debauchery? How so, friend friar?

The old man shook his head and wept anew. "Sir Knight, I've had carnal knowledge of many, many women. If I ever see the gates of heaven, 'twill be a greater miracle than the virgin birth."

I laughed to myself, certain that such a transgression would be easily forgiven with penitence. *Do not fret, Amadeaus, I am certain your way to heaven will not be barred.*

"Well, Sir Reynard, I hope you are right, but I fear my punishment will be dire," he said as he lay face down on the earth.

The mist was dissipating and the air smelled fresh once again. Where I saw no soldiers before, now the aisle was filled with men who appeared to be intoxicated. *What foul being did this?* I walked among them, nosing each one. Some seemed to rouse immediately, others remained groggy and only awoke as reluctantly, as a child reticent to attend his lessons. Amadeaus followed me and tried to awaken those I was unable to rouse.

I pawed Neeley's face. He awoke, startled, as is if he was unfamiliar with his surroundings. I did not reveal I could speak to the man, so I turned to Amadeaus, who quickly read my intent.

"Sir Neeley, have you an explanation for what occurred here?"

"Nay, good friar, one moment we were posted outside of the church as ordered by the King, the next it seemed that the church was afire. We formed a line and used our helmets to bring water from the stream to extinguish the blaze, but found none. No fire, just smoke. It stole our breath, we could not inhale clean air. I fell to the ground and knew nothing until the touch of yon fox's wet nose awakened me."

LADY CLARE

I was not overly concerned by Gwen's tirade. She'd banned me from Camelot so many times I'd lost count. But she knows I am the only one who will tell her the truth, the only one who will not grovel at her feet with a mouth full of lies.

She will come to me heart in hand and beg my forgiveness. In some areas, Guinevere had failed to mature. Oh, she was a beautiful woman, tall and statuesque, but she lacked some social skills and often let her anger rule her tongue.

Being a beautiful child she always got what she wanted and assumed it would be that way for all of her life. As she grew older and learned that was not the case, she often resorted to tantrums.

I continued my packing, as one never knew if this time she meant it. When I was nearly completed, I heard a soft knock on my door.

"Come in."

"Oh, Bess, I'm so sorry. You know I could never do without you. Please stay."

Gwen ran toward me and opened her arms. She'd been crying. "Please forgive me. I know I'm moody and selfish, but nobody wants me. Not Sir Bors, not Lancelot and certainly not my royal husband."

"Gwen you know that's not true. Arthur wants you by his side."

"Oh, he wants me by his side, as an ornament, not a wife. I'm decoration. He doesn't care how I think, what I like, or how I feel. 'Just sit there and look pretty, my lady.' Then he brings in this new golden child. She's prettier than I and I don't like it."

"Grow up, Gwen, she's an innocent child. She could never steal the heart of Arthur."

"I don't care about Arthur, what of all the others who use to vie for my attention?"

"Are you so shallow and such an infant that you want to be admired by all? Lady Guinevere is near the end of her tether. If she doesn't start acting like a queen, she may cease to be one. I was her best friend while we were growing up. We laughed, together, cried together, and discovered boys together. She seems to have never grown out of the trappings of youth."

"Perhaps you could show your husband how the child could be safely returned to the church? I know that is what she wants. You could befriend her and tell her, you will intercede with your husband to return her to her proper place, the Green Cathedral," I ventured. Surely somewhere beneath that silly attitude was the woman she was destined to be?

The Queen looked contrite, hung her head, and began to weep.

"You are right, Bess, I have been too self-centered and thinking only of my own comfort and amusement."

Without another word, Guinevere turned and left my tiny alcove. Then she looked over her shoulder and said, "Bess, keep packing."

QUEEN GUINEVERE

I can't believe I've been such an obnoxious fool. It is a wonder anyone even bothers to speak to me. All the harm I've caused so many, many people. Will God ever forgive me? Something must be done to right all these wrongs. I hurried down the marble corridor, taking care not to slip on the smooth surface.

"Arthur, Arthur," I cried as I entered his war room. Sliding into the room, I grasped the door handle to keep from falling. Arthur looked at me, his features contorted in puzzlement.

"Yes, Guinevere, what is it that you disturb me while I am conferring with my knights?"

Every man present turned to stare at me, even Sir Bors, whom I had insulted with my questions.

"I am truly sorry to interrupt you. I realize your meetings are critical to the well-being of your subjects, but I have a suggestion regarding the Green Cathedral you so generously constructed for me."

Arthur turned from the table and leaned against its edge, waving a hand he dismissed the men. I stood before him, my palms sweating, and my voice would not come forth. Finally I was able to speak.

"Y-Y-Your Highness, I beg your indulgence. It is truly sorry I am for my previous behavior and I would seek to be more of service to you and our people."

"Well, dear wife, this seems a great change in attitude. What is the cause of this?"

I hung my head. I knew I had not been the best of wives, but with Bess's help I think I can do better. "Bess, she pointed out I've been selfish and recently have been acting like a child."

"Bess is a most wise woman. I highly respect her. So what do you purpose regarding the Cathedral?" Arthur is a most through man, I dare not present him with silly ideas that amount to nothing. I would be wise as Bess, and put forth her suggestion.

"My dear friend thought it would be prudent to return Lila to the church accompanied by a knight and the two of us. Lila could inform me of what the workings of the church are and if there is any damage we three might be able to rectify it."

"That would seem to be a good plan, as I am concerned I've not heard from Neeley. Get ready, you and Bess. I'll inform Sir Bors and Lila. They, too, must prepare for the short journey."

"As you wish, My Lord."

I rushed back to the ladies' quarters and found Bess sitting on her bed crying. It was then I realized I'd not told her she was coming with me, when I told her to continue to pack."

I rushed to her side and put my arm around her shoulder. "Bess, why do you weep?"

"I never believed you would actually send me away, you always change your mind at the last moment. Gwen, we have been friends since we were children." She sniffed, and I handed her my handkerchief.

"You're right, Bess, I would never send you away, at least not without me." She looked up at me, a question in her gaze.

"I don't understand, you told me to pack. I am prepared to leave, but I fail to understand why."

"We are leaving together."

"Together? Has Arthur cast you aside?"

"No, but I wonder at my luck. He certainly has reason to, but we, you and I and Lila are going to the Green Cathedral. Sir Bors and his elite guard will be our escort. Arthur is concerned he's not heard from Officer Neeley, and he is worried something is amiss."

"Gwen, if something is wrong don't you think he would send more men?"

"Well, there are a number of knights there already. He thinks Sir Bors and his elite guard can set things aright."

"What of Lila? Does she know we are leaving?"

"I'm certain by now Arthur has informed both the lady and Sir Bors of our journey."

SIR BORS

I fail to understand how so much evil has entered this realm. Arthur formed this castle and country on the premise of good and honor. Why would anyone want to steal from a church?

I went into the life of a knight to be a fighter not a watcher of children. The Queen, though comely, is not a font of wisdom. When Arthur married her, I doubted the match would be long lived. Why in heaven's name would he send her back to the church? Furthermore, why would he encourage a friendship between his newly chosen Sentinel and his wayward queen?

I rode back to the end of our caravan and passed the three women in the opulent coach, who seemed to be in friendly conversation.

"Your Majesty, I wish to thank you for requesting of the King that I be permitted to return to my post. It is most important to me." Lila spoke softly and smiled meekly. It was clear to me she understood the full implications of this journey.

Guinevere shouted out the widow and demanded her mount. As she is the queen, my man accommodated her and brought her silver mare to the carriage.

Guinevere nodded, mounted, and clicked her horse's reins against its back, until she was riding faster than the coach. I moved along side of her and took her reins.

"Highness, there is a reason we are riding in the formation I chose and I would advise you not to alter it. It was set up for your protection. Now go back to your proper place."

She snatched the reins from me saying, "I will not. I am the Queen and I will ride wherever I choose."

Fortunately her lifelong friend spoke up.

"Gwen, grow up, the man is only doing as he is charged by the King. Stop being a petulant child."

"Who are you, dear Bess, to tell me what to do?"

"I am your friend. Though I sometimes wonder why."

"Excuse me, Sir Bors, perhaps if you clarified the reason for the formation, the queen might be more adaptable," Lila offered.

The girl was wise beyond her years and very diplomatic as well. I handed Guinevere's reins back. She sat quietly as I explained, the formations intent. Without the order, if we were attacked and it was all too common to be accosted, my men would not know how to defend her. Every person in the caravan had a place and a reason for that location. She listened then said, "I'm very sorry, I did not know how important my placement and that of the others was to the safety of the group." She dismounted, and I assisted her back into the conveyance.

We rode silently for about four miles. The day was turning to dark and though the church was near, I feared traveling in the twilight. I held up my hand and signaled the caravan to stop."

Lila seemed upset. "Sir Bors, we are very near the church, why must we stop so close?"

"I'm truly sorry, Lady Lila, but to travel so near an area where they are many pitfalls would be foolhardy. I cannot risk you, the queen, and Lady Clare, in an area I would not endanger even the most competent knight. My charge is to insure the safety of you ladies and my men. We will arrive early tomorrow."

"I understand, Sir Bors, but I am in need of replenishing my mendicants. I never travel without them. Might I venture to the nearby spring, where I might find some herbs I need?"

I noticed the bubbling spring as we neared the campsite. The herbs weren't far from the site, but I would not let her go unattended.

"Of course, Lady Lila, but you must be guarded. I will send a man with you."

"Really, Sir, that is not necessary as I need some private time as well."

"Very well, my man will attend you and remain out of sight has you do your necessaries. Then he will aid you with your harvesting."

Lila lowered her lashes and said softly, "Thank you, Sir Bors, I appreciate your discretion."

Chapter 4

GUINEVERE

"Bess, did you hear that?"

She wasn't paying attention, as usual. I heard it again, a muffled cry. "Lila!" I hollered. No response. But I was certain I heard a cry, and that it was Lila.

Sir Percival staggered toward me. "Where is Sir Bors? Someone struck me and Miss Lila is gone."

I took the soldier about his waist and led him to Sir Bors. I called out as we approached his tent, "Sir Bors, Sir Percival is injured." Bors emerged from the tent.

"Injured? How?"

"It's not serious, Sir, I was struck from behind. All I have is a big bump on the back of my head."

"Sit down, man, tell me all," the leader of the Elite Guard directed, as he motioned for a healer.

"I'm fine, Sir Bors, but, I lost the girl."

"What girl? Gwen and Bess are right here."

"Lady Lila, Sir, they've taken her."

"How did this happen, man? You were to be at her side at all times."

Percival hung his head, and I ran to his defense. It was not his fault, he'd only done what any gentleman would have done in his stead.

"Sir Bors, he is not to blame. He but turned his head as she did her necessaries." It was only a moment and she was snatched away. I begged the knight to allow me to go with the guard to find her. He denied my request. Under no circumstance would I be deterred by his response.

The men were busy preparing to hunt for the girl. They moved as an efficient machine. Yet, Sir Bors did not forget his duty.

"Your Highness, you and Lady Clare will remain here in the camp with Sir Percival and his guardsmen. My Queen, do not seek to defy my orders. It is my charge to keep you safe."

The knight knew me all too well. I would comply, at least appear to comply. I motioned to Bess to follow me into the tent. Watching her, I noted only one seemed to notice we went in the tent. But one was enough. He would tell the others. Waiting until all the men were about their tasks repairing armor and freeing it from rust. I looked peered out the rear of the tent. No one seemed to be looking this way.

Sir Bors was giving directions to his men. He seemed to be in entirely too preoccupied with the men's formation. He'd explained the importance of the configuration over and over. In my opinion, he was wasting valuable time.

"I'll find her myself, come on Bess." Easing out of the tent, I walked to the horses. They were all in a single line at the outskirts of the camp tethered to a strong rope. Fortunately ours were at the far end out of sight of the guards. I saddled my horse and Bess's as well. Walking the animals as quietly as possible, we did not mount until we were well out of sight. We rode in the direction we'd last seen Lila. As I could not hear any hoof beats, I dismounted.

"Gwen, get back on that horse, you know it's dangerous to be on foot." I got down close to the ground on one knee and parted the grass. "What are you doing now? Looking for bugs?"

"Don't be silly, Bess. I'm tracking. There is only one horse and its hoof prints are too deep for a single rider."

"So," Bess sighed, "How do you know how to track?"

"You should know as well, you've been on enough hunts. Don't you pay attention?"

"The only thing I pay attention to is how quickly the sun starts to set. You know I hate hunts."

I remounted and headed us in a Southerly direction. We cantered for a time as it was less harsh on our mounts, saving strength in case we needed to gallop.

I stopped the animal and held out my hand for Bess to stop as well. "Look, that's her. Come on." I slapped the reins to urge the animal to a faster gait.

At the sound of the oncoming hoof beats, the rider forced his mount to gallop as he held the girl.

Lila looked back frantically. When she saw who would be her rescuer, she knew she must assist, not merely sit and be a victim or all three of us would be captured.

I watched as Lila she eased her hand alongside of Damien's leg and freed his knife from his boot. She then reached back and drove the dirk into his thigh. Onward he pressed, seeming to be oblivious to the blood on his leg. However, his cries indicated he was sorely wounded. He drew his mount to a halt and extracted the knife from his thigh. Blood gushed from the wound and weakened, he lost his grip on Lila and his horse reared, then pounded back hard against the ground. Again, he reared, Lila clung to the saddle horn. The rider threw up his arms and fell forward onto the Sentinel.

I knew it was a good idea to have a sheath made for my bow. Silently I extracted it and a sharp steel from my quiver. My arrow landed cleanly in his neck.

"Bess, come her and help me get him off of her."

"My God, Gwen, what have you done?"

"What have I done? I killed the bastard."

"What will Arthur say? He may be one of the King's men."

"No, dear Bess, he wears not Arthur's colors. This man is a thief, a kidnapper. None of Arthur's men would commit such a foul deed. Now help me."

I stood on one side of the animal and tried to push the man's body from the horse. Bess got on the opposite side and together we shoved him to the ground.

"Lila, you are a very resourceful maid. Removing his knife was both timely and clever."

"Thank you, Your Majesty, that is high praise."

The lass seemed to be somewhat rattled, but she did not swoon, as many others would.

Chapter 5

AMADEAUS

I knew I was no longer a Sentinel, but still I felt the duty to restore what had been lost. Carefully, I extricated myself from the others and returned to the place that no longer was my charge. The brambles were still strewn about in untidy piles. I went to the shed and found an old rake.

The smaller pieces I raked into a neat pile and began to gather up the larger vines. I tugged at one that seemed to be wrapped around something. It would not give way, I pulled harder. Still nothing. Whatever it was, was firmly entrenched in the earth. Gathering the larger pieces I'd broken, I took them to the pile, when I noticed the sun was shining through the canopy. A single beam of sunlight glinted off of something within the bog that I had been unable to free from the ground. It was a deep green, so brilliant it may have actually been an emerald.

Could it be? Had the thieves removed it from the cross and found it impossible to remove from the church grounds? What strange occurrence this is. Who could it possibly be that could hold the gem and place it in a spot few would be able to access?

Driven from my thoughts by the sound of hoof beats I turned and saw a large draft horse without a rider approach. If he's tame, perhaps I can use him to free the large green stone. Slowly and quietly I walked toward the animal. It hung its head, there were whip marks all along its flank. Whoever owned the animal certainly hadn't cared for him properly. He let me touch him and I rubbed his muzzle and spoke softly to him.

He nickered and trotted toward a large fern at the edge of the bog. The morning sun again caught the reflective gleam of eyes, hidden within the greenery.

The fox emerged. He seemed angry as he growled, not at me, but a simple display of anger.

Amadeus, do you know who did this to my horse?

"Reynard! Is it truly you? Where have you been?"

I've been here all along. I got tired and laid down to take a nap. I see you've found Duncan or perhaps he found you.

"This is your horse? Why then has the animal been so mal treated? It does not seem the thing Sir Reynard would do."

You're quite right. When I owned Duncan, he was groomed daily to a sheen on his coat and his mane had nary a tangle.

"When you owned him? How did you lose him?"

I lost him for the same reason I am no longer a Sentinel. Wagering.

"Well, my friend we all have our vices."

Our conversation was interrupted by the sounds of hoof beats. Amedeaus raised his arms to halt the approaching horsemen, lest they come to close to the swampy area. The party consisted of Sir Bors, Sir Percival, their men, and the three women, Lila, the Queen, and her lady-in-waiting, Lady Clare.

I was not surprised to see them. The problem would resolve itself of this, I was most certain. Apparently I was the only one who welcomed the group. Reynard eyed the men suspiciously. He walked around the men, glaring at Sir Percival, as if challenging him to a duel.

The knight did not respond, but moved to help the women to dismount. He first aided the Queen, then Lady Clare. When he went to assist Lila, Reynard stepped between her and the knight. He bared his teeth and growled softly. Lila slid from her mount and reached down to pet Reynard. Sir Percival apparently sensing she was in danger from the wild animal, slapped her hand from the foxes head.

Lila was angered by the knight's action.

"Sir Percival, there is not cause for you to strike my hand away from petting the fox. I know this animal well. Do not think to do that again." She turned her back on him and came to my side. Percival was not deterred in the least and followed her.

Sir Bors directed his men to assist in the cleanup then came to my side.

He whispered, "What of the stone? Has it been stolen?"

"Nay it is over there in the bog," I replied.

"I think it has some capability to protect itself from being removed from here."

"But how could that be? It's a stone."

"True, but it is a sacred stone."

I was then distracted by Reynard's low, guttural growl. He was pacing back and forth in front of Sir Percival. Percival was oblivious to the animal, but he did show affection for Lila. This was what truly angered Reynard.

Percival assessed the situation and asked me if I had sufficient rope to wrap around the stone and leave a length to pull upon. The amount I had would not encircle the stone.

"Sir Percival, I fear I do not have long enough rope to do the task. Do any of the men have rope?"

Sir Bors joined the discussion. "We do not have a single piece but each of the men have enough rope to pitch their tents. If we tie them all together I am certain the length would suffice."

All the men searched their gear. Each extricated a length and joined it to the rope that was passed from man to man. Quickly a length was reached that would encircle the stone.

Sir Percival threw it as close to the bog as he could. He then started to enter the swampy ground. Reynard stood in front of him and growled. It was clear the two did not like each other. But this time the fox was warning the foolish knight.

Sir Bors interjected, "Percival, the ground is not stable enough for someone of your weight to step on. Reynard will take the rope to the stone —"

"Who is Reynard? Is it someone who frequently enter such bogs as this?"

I was reluctant to reveal the fox's true identity. Rather than have to explain the animal's existence, Reynard brushed past me and took up the piece of rope. Carefully holding the rope in his mouth, he crept slowly to the edge of the stone and with his snout he pushed the fibers beneath the green stone. He then went to the far side of the gem and began to dig at the opposite edge. It took some time but finally, Reynard pulled the cord from underneath the stone and looked toward Lila. She looked to me for instruction.

"Lila, you are the lightest of us. Reynard wants you to come to him and secure the knot around the rock. He will protect and guide you. Fear not, he knows well the danger of the shifting ground." The lass proceeded to walk toward the fox.

Reynard barked and went down on his front paws. He did this several times before I realized he meant for the girl to crawl to him on her hands and knees, thus distributing her weight over a larger surface. She would then be less likely to be sucked into the more. Understanding far better than I for at his first action she was already down and crawling slowly toward the stone.

REYNARD

Why this fool thinks he should be the director of Lila baffles me. He has the intelligence of stable dung. That she is able to understand me is proof we are destined to be mates. How that will be established is beyond my ken but feel within my heart it will somehow be made aright.

After securing the rope, she handed it to me and backed out on hands and knees from the marshy ground. The smile she gave me would light several cathedrals.

Amedeaus, take Percival's saddle and place it on Duncan. He will be calm for you now.

Amedeaus nodded and went to Percival's mount. The large warhorse was none too docile. He stamped his massive hooves and snorted.

"Sir Percival, come assist me," the cleric ordered.

"You have no right to give me orders." the knight balked.

"Percival," Sir Bors shouted, "You will take orders from this man, or I shall be happy to inform the King you're insubordinate."

"But, he is not a man of the military. I should not have to take orders from a Druid. He's not even Christian."

"His beliefs are none of your concern. He is accountable only to Arthur. You will follow his directions. Now move and get that saddle."

Not certain I could laugh since I was an animal, my chuckle warmed me to my very bones. The knight reluctantly did as he was bid.

Amedeaus, place the saddle on Duncan. Once you have it in place and cinched tightly secure the end of the rope around the pommel. In fact, wind it around both pommels. It will give a more even pull.

Sir Bors interjected, "Percival do you have an extra chinch strap? That horse is far larger than yours."

"I noticed," the man sullenly replied.

"I have sufficient chinch on my saddle as I use it on several different mounts."

When the saddle was in place, Sir Percival went to mount Duncan. The horse bared his teeth and snapped at the knight. I was pleased my horse did not like him. Crouching low, I bent to get the most height from my jump onto the saddle. In one swift move, I was atop my horse. I bent low and whispered to Duncan, *Pull back, Dunc, slow and steady, no sudden movement as the rope might snap.*

The horse snorted and stamped his hooves. He was unaccustomed to hearing my voice from the body of a fox. Finally he settled. He recognized my order, even though he did not know my present form. He began to pull, as firm, strong, and straight as a machine. With each step backward, the stone began to rise form the muck. Finally the stone was on solid ground.

I turned to Amadeus and told him to direct Duncan to bring the stone as close to the cathedral as possible. The horse quickly responded to the Druid's instruction. Once the gem was pulled across solid earth, it created a green path, where the grass grew thick and lush. Duncan was eager to be free of the rope and eat of the vegetation. The other horses followed along grazing. The smell was so enticing, I, too, jumped down and nibbled at the intoxicating blades of grass.

I usually ate of grass only when I have stomach distress. This time, however, the scent was what drew me. All at once I developed and acute pain in my gut. It hurt like blazes. The remedy had become the malady. I fell to the ground, closed my eyes, and doubled into a ball.

I'd never known such pain as either fox or man. Certain I was in death throes, I needed to find Lila. She must know of my feelings before I die. I opened my eyes and found she was above me, trying to comfort me. She was petting me, concern in her touch. For some reason she stayed her hand and was staring at it. I looked at her and noted that the fur was bright red on her palm. It was mine. What was happening to me? I turned my head and tried to lick my shoulder. My mouth tasted my own fur. It was coming off of me. Why? How? I looked to the Queen. Her mouth hung open in astonishment, the Lady Clare did likewise, but Lila seemed to almost expect the phenomena.

I began to shiver. I was colder than I had ever been. I felt the marrow in my bones congeal. My blood was moving at the pace of a snail.

Someone shouted, "Give him a plaid, he's naked. Build a fire quickly. We have to warm him else he will die."

The voice was frantic, and I realized it was Lila. *She was worried about me? Knowing she might return my feelings created a small warm spot deep within my core. There was definitely some changes going on within my body. What could be the cause for this transformation? Was I being rewarded for securing the stone? Did I dare hope the change would be permanent?*

Percival came over to the group that was tending me. "What kind of trick is this, Druid?"

Amadeaus looked up at the knight, anger in his glance.

"This is not a trick, you fool. Don't you recognize destiny when it stares you in the face? This is nothing I have done, nor in truth, that any man has done. This is divine intervention. I know not what divinity, but the event comes from some force outside my ken."

I didn't like the man merely on principle, but his presence is permeated by suspicion. He was all too attentive to Lila. She wrapped the plaid closely around me and began to rub my hands.

Warmer now, I dared to speak. "Lila, thank you for your concern, I thought I was going to die without you knowing how deeply I care for you." That I was able to speak aloud and was understood by all was a miracle in itself.

Sir Percival did not react, as I thought he would, by my transformation, yet thought it reason to take Lila from me.

"Come away, Lila, this can only be the work of something foul," he said, pulling her from my arms.

"Sir Percival," Sir Bors shouted.

"Leave the lady alone. She is not your charge."

"I'll not leave this woman, to be corrupted by this evil minion of the devil." the knight retorted.

"I shall take care of her."

"You shall not. That is an order."

"But, Sir?" Percival whined. It was clear his commanding officer was displeased with him.

I was glad Sir Bors took his stand, but I would not allow the simpering fool to think I needed the knight's protection. Standing, I drew the plaid tightly around my hips and took the other a generous knight held out to me. This I wrapped over my shoulders. I marched over to Sir Percival. Poking him in the chest, I said, "You harebrained nincompoop, you are not to ever touch this lady's person. Do. You. Understand?"

As my anger grew, I noted my nose seemed to be growing. It was turning into a muzzle. Why? I rather like being a man. As I contemplated the situation, my ire cooled. Calm once again my snout retreated into my face becoming a nose once again. So great was my relief I grabbed Lila and swung her around.

She gasped for breath and said, "Put me down." As she struck my face with a slap so gentle as to be called a caress, I gently set her down.

Amadeaus came to my side and pried the girl from my arms.

"Reynard, we have much to do we must replace the stone and you must learn to control your temper. Apparently anger causes you to become a fox."

Chapter 6

BLACK DUFF

Why did I ever let my guard down with my sister? I know she's evil to the marrow. Even when we were children, whatever another child had she wanted, she made sure she got it. She was no child when she stole my horse. I had planned to return the animal to Sir Reynard when he raised the money to buy him back. I didn't want the money for myself. The plan was to find a mare and mate it with the stallion. The knight earned my respect and I thought the two of us could raise exceptional horses when we were too old to compete in tournaments.

Well, that dream went up in smoke. The moment Natheria saw him, she demanded I give him to her. When I refused, she had that weasel Percival ambush me and throw me in this rotten hole of a dungeon. Today is supposed to be my hanging. I have no hope of rescue. Few know here I am and fewer care. I wish I had been able to return Reynard's horse. It was the one blemish on my record. The other person was always my first thought. Be it a servant, a colleague, or even one of my animals, their needs always preceded my own. It was the code I lived by.

NATHERIA

The hours I spent lurking around this damned swamp seem to have been in vain. My knees are cramped from kneeling just outside their view. I need to know if there is some trick to getting the stone off the Cathedral grounds. When my men pried it from the cross, I thought I'd won. They pulled it outside and it rolled right into the bog. As I saw it sink, my hopes sunk with it. I have to have that gem.

It was not my finest hour and Sir Percival was of little or no help. He owed me and owed me much. I saved him from persecution when he tried to capture the Queen. The idiot thought he would get away with stealing Arthur's bride. He was her escort to Camelot, when the King took her to wed.

If not for that love-struck Lancelot, saving the day by demanding he escort the lady, Percival would be in Arthur's dungeon.

If only Duff would be my ally, but no, he had to be honorable. Him and his tournaments, bah. Why compete for wealth when you can simply take it? And that stone is worth more than I can calculate. I must have it. I will have it. Neither the fool knight nor my idiot brother will stop me.

Though still in my cramped spot, I saw activity. They were moving the stone with tent ropes. *Why didn't I think of that? I had enough men to pull it free, but I am certain it has some spell or something on it.* It rolled into the morass more of its own volition. There was more here than what I saw, than what I comprehend.

That fox, or should I say half fox, has some magical properties. I motioned for my man who was standing watch with me, to take the fox when no one was looking. It would not be an easy task. All of the soldiers seemed intent upon replacing the stone into the cross and did not notice the half-transformed fox shaking his head and gnashing his teeth. The object of his ire was Percival. *I was none too happy with the fool either.* The creature was so angered by the knight, yet the morphing of the fox was not complete.

"Grab him," I shouted to my watchman, "He's weak and disoriented by his change."

Hum, perhaps this watchman is due a raise. He captured the fox and secured his muzzle so he could not cry out to his friends. I am well pleased with the man. To have the forethought to silence the creature was masterful.

"Sir," I said, sidling next to the man.

"You have pleased me greatly. I shall find some way to compensate you."

He did not respond as I expected, but nodded and held the animal tightly. "Anger him further if you can then take him to the dungeon and put him with my brother. Maybe we can learn from them."

REYNARD

Damn, I hate to be coddled like a pet. *Put me down, you numbskull.*

"Of course, Captain," the soldier answered immediately.

He actually heard me? Then he set me on the ground and advised me not to become angry.

Not get angry? Well, damn it I am angry.

"How would you like to have your life taken from you for some misdeed long passed?"

"I understand, Captain Reynard. But if you are to get out of here, you'll need a calm head. The man turned. "The jailer is coming, I have to leave you. Remember, no matter what happens you must not show anger."

The jailer approached, his keys bounding off his massive stomach. His girth would not allow him to actually enter the cell.

"You there!" he yelled to the fellow who just placed me on the floor.

"Lady N wants ter see ya right now. Gets a move on."

I'm in an internal rage, but I must not give in to it. Though I dislike being told what to do, the man's advice was sound. He stepped from the cell and saluted me. Why?

"Well, Reynard, don't you know the man?" Duff asked.

"No, should I?"

"Yes, you should he's one of your officers. Don't you know me? We once competed in a horse race." Apparently my face showed some sign of recognition, as he smiled.

Much calmer I stared at the man. One of my men working for this foul woman? I cannot believe one of my men would behave in such a manner. Yet, he was familiar, I recognized the stance if not the man. His clothes were unlike any other I had seen before. I combed my memory. In a flash, it came to me.

"My God, that was Neeley. No wonder he saluted."

"Yes, it is, but do not allow anyone else to know that you were once his commander. He will help us get out of here."

"You seem familiar. Do I know you as well?"

"You should, I won your horse from you."

"Duff, I should be mad at you, but I am finding my ire is causing me a disservice. What happened to my horse? Just a short while ago, I saw him and he was sore maltreated. I did not take you for the type of man that would abuse an animal."

"I'm not. Duncan was stolen from me."

"Do you know who took him?"

"I do. It was my sister, the very one who has thrown us in this damp, dark dungeon. She gives me little food and nothing to cover myself when I try to sleep."

"That is highly irregular. Most siblings care for one another. Why did she steal from her own brother?"

"She steals whatever takes her fancy. Since Duncan is such a remarkable horse, she felt he would bring a great price. It wasn't the animal she wanted, only its value. She gleefully informed me yesterday the animal left her shortly after she acquired him. I don't think he was happy with her treatment. His wounds have healed and Duncan responds well, unless he's forced to go against all he's been taught before. Natheria made ridiculous demands. She wanted him to stand on his hind legs for long periods of time. When he was unable to stand in that fashion, she became angered and beat him."

How could anyone treat an animal so cruelly? The more I thought about it, the madder I got. I started to pace back and forth, my teeth clenched so tightly my jaw hurt.

"Calm down, man, can't your see what you are doing to yourself?"

My anger again caused me to become more fox than man. "Thanks, Duff, I'm not generally known for my quiet demeanor." I continued my pacing, with each step, I decreased my fury. Close to the door, I turned and caught my toe on something in the dirt. Reaching down I discovered the ground was hard packed, with the small exception of a spot near the edge of the the cell. I scrapped the area around the protrusion and finally was able to extricate a rather large rusted key.

Duff inquired, "What have you found?"

"Luck must be with us. It's a key. I think it might be the key to this cell."

"Great, but how did it get here? Could it be a trap?"

"I suppose it could be, but it is more likely that it was left by Neeley."

"Possible. He's never seemed to be the kind of a man my sister would employ. You appear to know the man. How do you read this situation?"

"Neeley is one of my most trusted men. I would trust him with my life."

"Well, that's good because that is what is happening."

I heard a noise and motioned to Duff to be silent. Within the dungeon there was little light, just enough to see the outline of a person. The rotund jailer returned with a bucket of porridge. He bent to open the cell door, set the bucket on the floor, and pushed it into the cell with his foot. Following the sound of the bucket scraping the ground, I heard a loud thud. The jailer fell to the ground.

"Neeley, why are here? Is the key your doing?"

"Of course. Now use it and let's get out of here. I'd like to put him in the cell, but I'm sure he won't fit. I hit him quite hard, he'll be out a while. Won't give us much of a lead, but it is better than nothing. Come on."

Neeley led us through a maze of sorts. The passageway was dark and dank, smelling like month-old fish. It was a good thing he is here to show us the way. Without him I would certainly have gotten lost. Finally the stench grew less odious. I smelled salt. We were near the sea. Up ahead I saw a fluffy white cloud in a sky of bright blue. We were truly free.

"Where are we? And tell me, Neeley, it seems to me that not long ago I saw you at the church. How is it you are working for Natheria? You never impressed me as a traitor."

"Trust me, Reynard, I am no traitor. I am here at the King's bidding. I've been able to sneak away from Natheria from time to time which is how I saw you at the church. I have been watching the cathedral trying to learn what it is the witch wants with the cross. Arthur believes she has a distorted view of its value. I, on the other hand, think her avarice is more for power than riches."

Duff, who had been eerily quiet since we left the cell, spoke up, "That makes sense. She always wants control. Control over everyone and everything. Even as a child, she was bossy."

NATHERIA

I'm sick of being in this cramped stinking mire. I just wish someone would reveal something useful. I went from my hidden location and moved toward the edge of the church grounds, Percival was going away from the men. Perhaps the fool remembered he works for me? I hissed into the air, "Percival, come here."

He looked up and appeared confused. Unable to locate the direction of the sound.

I hissed again, "Percival. Over here. Come to me."

"And why should I come to you? You are not my master and I am slave to no man or woman."

"Because I pay you, you twit."

"Come now, Natheria, you know there are more reasons than pay that draw you to me. Face it, you need me."

His arrogance knows no bounds. He is comely but that is not what his largest attraction is. Loyalties can be bought, and fortunately I have greater coin than Sir Bors. I realize that could change if I fail in this endeavor.

"Have you learned anything that will actually aid me? Or are you wasting your time trying to gain the favor of the little church girl?"

"Yes, Lady, I do seek her favor. Not for myself, but to garner the information you require."

"You would do better listening, rather than following her about like a love-sick calf."

"I report all to you. What I do in my personal time is none of your affair."

"Percival, you are a poor excuse for a man. Can't you do anything I tell you, in the way I tell you?"

"Madam, I am well-schooled in the ways of espionage, I know what I am doing. I was coming to give you my findings."

"Coming to me? Then why are you headed away from me? Don't you think to cross me, knight, for in any altercation you will not get the better of me. I have not gained all I have by being foolhardy. Tread lightly, Percival, you are not indispensable. I can replace you with a river rock."

"Lady, I think you will re-evaluate my worth to you when I tell you, I know of the ritual that releases the stone. Other than the girl, I am the only one who knows of it."

Surely the Druid knows of the incantation, for he, too, was a sentinel. Perhaps, Percival had never seen him perform the rite. The man is filled with self-importance.

From across the mire I saw the lass Lila kneel at the edge and lower her head. "There, see she does it, even now. Watch," Percival ordered. "I do not like being given orders especially from an underling, but I did as he suggested. Once again, I crouched in the vegetation, pulling the knight down with me. She was mumbling something, I could not make out what she was saying. The more intently I listened, I realized this was the same sound the Druid made when I first learned of the cross. *Perhaps they were part of a secret society?*

She started to rise and Percival slowly moved around the mire and came up behind her. Shying away from him, she drew her shawl tightly around her shoulders. I could not tell if she was afraid of him or merely disgusted with him. He reached for her and she wrenched her elbow from him, then drew it back and punched him in the stomach. Percival was not deterred. He grabbed her tightly and lifted her off the ground.

"Put me down, you snake. I'm not interested in you. Your attentions are not wanted. Leave me be. Let me down at once."

The fool pointed at me. "See her there? She wishes to speak with you on a matter of great import."

I rose from my position, trying to show as much majesty as possible. I smoothed my gown and shook off the dirt from the hem. "Young lady, from whence do you come? You appear to be a woman of some consequence. What is your position in this church?"

The girl was clearly frightened. Good, it made my task easier.

Intimidation is a wonderful tool.

"Set her down Percival, she's a smart girl she will not flee. Will you, my child?"

Damn it, she did, as quick as a frog snares a fly. Well, she won't get away with it.

She scuttled on all fours to the far side of the bog. More fearful of Percival she did not break eye contact with him. To my advantage, carefully and quietly I moved to the far edge of the mire, and snuck up behind her and grasped her firmly. She fought me vigorously, kicking, screaming, and wiggling as furiously as a bass above water. Fortunately, I am rather large for a woman. I stand at six feet, and weigh several stone. She would not escape my clutches.

"Percival, you incompetent twit, bring me some rope."

"We are not going to learn anything if you hold her prisoner, she has to be coerced to our manner of thinking. In a sense we have to woo her. She has to trust us."

"You know, Percival, you may think you are a brilliant tactician, but all your schemes are as mere wisps in the wind. Now bring me the rope and bind her hands. She is going to visit my brother and the fox man."

"You can't throw her in the dungeon, she'll never talk if you send her there."

Perhaps he is right. "All right, lock her in the tower. She won't be able to get out but, the room is more than comfortable."

Percival smiled.

Probably thought he had bested me. We'll see about that. He bound her hands and led her to my modest castle. The girl was becoming more and more fearful, she began to whimper. I stepped forward, so I was walking along side of her.

"Fear not, lass, you shan't be harmed. Just tell us of the ritual and you will be released."

Percival put his arm about her shoulders, leaned down, and whispered in her ear. Obviously he did not wish me to hear, but my hearing is as unusual as my size. I heard every word. *So he would free her from my clutches? I think not.*

"You see, young miss, you shall be quite comfortable in the tower. It is well appointed and quite cozy. Should you require anything, simply pull on the bell cord and someone will come to assist you. The heavy tapestry ribbon that hangs in the corner by the fireplace will ring a bell in the kitchen.

The poor girl was frightened, but I had to have the incantation. There was no other way. "We'll leave you now to rest. At dinner, I will have a plate brought to you. Not prisoner fare, the same as is served at my table."

I grabbed Percival's arm and nodded for Neeley to take her to her quarters. "You fool, you are not her paramour? She certainly has no feelings for you other than hatred."

Percival glared at me, saying, "Under better circumstances she would fall into my arms."

"Listen, Percy, while you are fair of face you are no lothario. You couldn't woo that woman if you had gold coming out of your ears."

"Have a care, Natheria, you are not to address me as such. I shall not only woo her I shall win her and gain the secret before you."

"I think not, foolish knight. Lila may be a lady of the church, but she is not ignorant in the ways of evil men."

PERCIVAL

If that woman didn't have so much power, I would gladly crush her larynx, so I would never again have to listen to her nattering away at everything. I will have that lass in my arms in less than a fortnight.

I left the castle and went to the nearby town to find some trinkets and scented soap. For some reason every woman I've ever known loves such things. Women are so easy to flatter. Little Lila will succumb to my attentions.

I left my horse at the edge of town and walked along the narrow street of shops. The sign of a silversmith caught my eye. As I looked over his wares, I noted a unique piece. A tiny cross, wrought of silver with a green stone at the center. Most assuredly Lila would be impressed by this piece. It was on a twisted chain that looked like a braided vine.

I'm sure she will be reminded of the cross at the cathedral, and believing I revere it as much as she, perhaps she will tell me of the incantation.

"Good Sir, would you kindly wrap up that cross?" I pointed to the item and watched as he removed it from his display case. He placed it in a royal purple velvet sack, drew the ties together and handed it to me.

"That will be six pence, Sir Knight. May your lady wear it in good health and joy."

As I handed him the coin, I pondered that the joy would be mine. All mine and perhaps if she is enamored of the gift as well as the giver, she too will be mine. I know Natheria thinks she has my heart, but she is sorely mistaken. The girl is far more comely and suits my taste perfectly.

I was not gone overly long, yet hoped my brief absence would allow the lady to settle into her quarters. My only concern was that Natheria had not investigated the tower room before she sent Lila there. I'd made subtle changes that Lila would be sure to appreciate. Yet I did not want Natheria to be aware of the luxuries I'd provided for her prisoner. As I approached the edge of the town, I noted a small vineyard. Some sweet wine would be another incentive for the little church lady. I had to be careful for if I lost myself to the lady's charms, I might forget my mission. Above all I must keep a clear head and not allow her to be frightened.

By the time I reached the castle, the evening was near upon me. The last visages of the sun colored the sky with soft pinks, vivid oranges, and a muted purple as dusk descended into dark.

I noted a light from the tower room. Hopefully someone had started a fire for Lila. The light I saw was a mere candle glow to pierce the darkness. I don't imagine she was afeard of the dark, she was not a child, but surely she should have the comfort of a fire as the evenings were growing colder with the impending autumn.

I rode across the bailey, dismounted, and handed my reins to a stable boy. Handing him my parcel, I directed him to place it in my quarters. Entering the great hall, I spied Natheria sitting on a large chair on the dais. One of her legs was carelessly hung over the arm of the chair. A most undignified pose. How such a powerful woman could be so crass, escaped me. She had all the dignity of a tavern wench. Her dress was wrinkled and her eyes drawn to mere slits. As I drew near, I realized she was drunk and mumbling incoherently, something about Lila. At least the lass's name was the only word I could clearly decipher. By the saints, I hope she has not seen the tower room.

"Sa bout time you returned. Where ya been? You some kinda spy? You still owe allegiance to Arthur? After all, he did knight you. Don't know why, yer stupid."

"Not entirely stupid, my lady, I was fetching us some sweet wine to celebrate our capture of the church girl."

She was holding a mug with a handle, twisting it around her finger. "Well, fill it up. And hurry up about it."

"I've had the wine sent to my quarters, I was not sure you hadn't already retired for the night. Bowing briefly, I went to the stairs. My intention for the wine had been changed. Now I wished I'd purchased two bottles. But for now, one would suffice. I'm sure the necklace would be more welcomed than wine by Lady Lila.

Hurrying down to the great room, I saw Natheria, head lolled back and the mug swinging from her finger. She was out cold. This would work to my advantage. I took the mug and gently lifted the woman into my arms. Her head fell against my chest. She tried to say something and kissed my throat with wet, sloppy kisses. I tried to hide my revulsion and gently brushed her hair from her face. She smiled a drunken wobbly grin, I could only hope she would not remember the exact events of this evening. I will weave her a tale that will convince her I am the answer to her prayers that she cannot do without me. Domination is a powerful aphrodisiac.

I took her to her bed and laid her there, even as slumber softened the hard lines of her face, she was not a pretty woman. Though she had the power to enchant me beyond reason.

Eager to be with the woman of my choice, I left Natheria and made haste to the tower. Natheria had posted a guard, the new man, Neeley. He did not impress me, always butting in where he was not wanted.

"Thank you, Neeley, you are no longer needed, I'll take over."

"Is this per Natheria's direction?"

"It is."

"As you wish, Sir Percival. Should you have need of me, I'll be in the barracks."

"I shall send for you if you are needed." I did not like the tone of his voice or his demeanor. He acted as if he'd caught me in a wrongdoing. *What I do, right or wrong is none of his business.*

I tapped gently at the door. There was no invitation to enter. Carefully I pushed open the door. The room seemed empty, but I then noticed a small rise in the bed furs. She was sleeping and had not heard my knock.

I walked to the edge of the bed and placed my hand on her shoulder, which was bare above the coverings. She jumped, grabbing the furs tightly around her.

"Get out," she cried.

"I'll not suffer further indignities from the likes of you."

"But, my dear Lady Lila, you have suffered no hurt or humiliation from me. 'Tis all the fault of Natheria. I am here to protect you." The look in her eyes indicated, I was the last person she wanted protecting her. She backed away from me to sit in the chair by the hearth, then drew her knees to her chest and glared at me.

"My lady, I swear to you upon my oath as a knight no harm shall come to you from me. All I desire from you is to be your friend.

Nothing less nothing more." Somehow I had to convince her. I turned away and walked toward the door. "If you do not wish me to protect you, there is nothing else I can offer you." I had my hand on the latch when she called to me.

"Sir Percival, please stay."

Clearly she was wary, but she was softening toward me. "I guess I have to believe you. For you have not laid a hand upon me. But, Sir Percival, remember your code as a knight."

"For a certainty, I am taken aback that you would believe otherwise." I moved closer to her and gently guided her to the brocade chaise near the window. "Come, my dear, sit and enjoy the view."

She sat near the edge of the seat, not leaving enough room for me to sit beside her.

"Lady Lila, please move aside so I too may savor the scenery. Today is such a fine one not to enjoy."

She looked up timidly, nodded and moved aside to allow me to sit next to her. The birds were singing and the crisp autumn air wafted carrying the scent of impending winter. The tower was quite warm, but the open window cooled the room. I rose and went to the bed to remove one of the furs. I placed it around her shoulders, hugging her as I did so. She did not rebuff me. Once again, I sat. I wrapped both arms around her and pulled her body to mine. I tried to lift her chin that I might kiss her, when she resisted. She pushed me away and screamed, "Get away, you brute. How dare you attempt to compromise me?"

Before I could answer, the door was flung open and Neeley came to her rescue.

"Lady Lila, are you injured? Has this man forced himself upon your person?"

"No, Neeley, I am not hurt, just embarrassed that a knight would behave in such a manner."

"He'll not do that again. Will you, Percy?"

I lunged at him, sword drawn. This fool would not get the best of me. He avoided my thrust and parried with one of his own. It had to be luck that he nicked my elbow. He was moving more like a knight than a watchman. I stopped to catch my breath and lowered my head, suddenly I was struck from behind. I fell to the floor.

NEELEY

Wow, that little lady packs quite a wallop. "Lila, thanks for the assist, but I am sure I could have handled him."

She panted, trying to regain her breath. "I'm sure you would have, but he made me so damn mad, I've been thinking all day of hitting him. It wasn't until I saw the cauldron that I found a suitable weapon."

I smiled. The girl was right, if any one ever deserved being hit with an iron pot it was Percy. Never before had I heard her swear, she was good and truly angry.

"Lila, we must leave at once. He will be out for a while, but we haven't much time. We have to get you back to the Cathedral"

She was frightened and held the fur tightly around her.

"But I have no clothes, I can't run in just a fur."

"I foresaw that and procured you clothes. They are not yours, but will suffice. I had boots made for you some time ago as I was certain this situation would arise."

"You had boots made for me? Why?"

"With the change in the weather you will need sturdy boots. I knew Natheria would allow you only slippers, so I have provided the 'running shoes'."

"Dress quickly and then follow me. Where we are going is not an easy path and you must stay close to me. Do you understand?"

"I do. I shall follow your direction." I was surprised how quickly she dressed, and now was pulling on the boots.

She stood, still holding the fur. "I think we might have use for this as evenings are growing chillier by the hour. I know I shouldn't take it, but he should not have tried to compromise me."

Laughing, I said, "I think the loss of the fur will bother Natheria far less than the loss of you."

As I slipped into the tunnel, I heard Lila say, "Neeley, where are you?" I reached behind me and took her hand.

She gasped and held my hand tightly. "Thank God, I feared I dreamt you had come to save me."

We moved along the corridor in darkness. Lila did not complain, simply firmly held my hand.

"Lila, I am not going to leave you, but I must have the use of both hands, to light this torch. I'd left it there when I led Sir Bors and Sir Reynard to their freedom. Fortunately I counted the steps so knew exactly where to find the firebrand.

I felt her set my hand free, but in that same moment, she placed her palm on my shoulder. She was not fearful only prudent. Striking a flint against my knife the light burst into flame.

The way through the tunnel was far shorter than it was for the men as we started closer to the end. When we emerged, it was fairly near the Cathedral. Lila recognized the area and raced ahead of me.

Reynard was now a man. The man I served under, my friend and commander.

NATHERIA

I knew that Neeley did not have my interests in mind when he came to work for me. But, he was comely and I felt I could win him over to my cause. However, he, too, was noble. He and my brother shared the same values.

Neeley failed to close the panel completely when he purloined my hostage. Did he think I did not know of the passageways of my own castle? Foolish, foolish man. If you were only as cunning as you are handsome.

I knew without a doubt Neeley would take her back to the church. Where she would be protected. Again, you are foolish. I took a different route than they and arrived at the church just ahead of them. My men followed closely and were in position before Neeley and Lila arrived.

Reynard rushed to greet her and swept her up in his arms. Lila was overcome to the point of fainting. Reynard led her to a large rock near the edge of the bog, seated her, and began to console her. She cried and cried and buried her head in his shoulder.

"Wait here," the fox man said. He rose and left the girl unattended. Moving to his tent, he did not look back and the lass fainted. My brother noticed her swoon and rushed to her side.

I hissed, hoping only my brother would notice and acknowledge my presence. But Duff was not interested in anything other than the girl and his friend Reynard.

The captain seemed to resent my brother holding his lady. As he hastened to her side, he shoved Duff aside.

Duff stood and smiled at Reynard. "Foolish man, I have no interest in the lady I only prevented her from falling to the ground."

"I'm sorry, Duff, all of this has me quite on edge. Being two different species, falling in love with Lila and trying to save the church. It's a lot to take in."

"Well, I'm sure you will have the resources you need to see you through."

Percival was observing, his face a grotesque mask of hatred. I moved into the bushes. I did not wish to be seen. Percival was a loose cannon. When he is angry, he loses his reason. At one time he was considered a brilliant tactician. I edged my way around the mire and grabbed his sleeve.

"What do you want?" he snarled.

"No thanks to you, I may have lost her."

"Percival, you have lost sight of our goal. She is not to be your wife. We simply need the incantation."

"Trust me, oh foolish one, they will scramble like rats from a sinking ship. Lila will rush to the sanctuary to save the scriptures and the others will be so concerned with the fire they will not notice her."

"I see what is it you want me to do? Do I encircle the bog with the torch?"

"There is no need for that, I've set a fuse. I don't want to risk you being seen."

I'm sure it is not my person she fears revealed. All she cares about is her plan not being foiled.

I needed a diversion, something to take their main concern from the girl. I'd learned that this bog was not only a hazard if one stepped into it, but frequently gave off highly flammable gases. The gases would not ignite unless a flame was introduced, and over time, I'd learned to control the flame. I spent many hours when the land around the church was unguarded, perfecting my control until I could manipulate the gases to my will. Somehow, I knew the information would prove useful.

Grabbing Percival's sleeve, I ordered him to fetch a flame from the castle. It needed to be made of pitch, not a simple flint-started ignition. He wrenched away from me.

"There is no sense fetching a flame. Face it, woman, you are finished in this endeavor. You'll not get your incantation and I shall not have the woman I love. Begone from me. I will not follow your biddings, nor will I remain with you. That should convince her, she needs me."

"I suggest you rethink that, gentle knight. Arthur would be sooo pleased to learn of the knight of his round table that was less than chivalrous. Do you understand, Percy?"

"Don't call me that. I've not disgraced my honor following the woman I love. Even Arthur would recognize the importance of love."

"I'll call you whatever I wish, and do not think Arthur to be so gullible to believe all you do, you do in the name of love."

"All right, I'll get a torch."

"Make certain there is sufficient pitch on it and do not light it until you are once again back here. Understand Percy?"

PERCIVAL

Though I once thirsted for the power Natheria offered, this was no longer the case. I've fallen hopelessly in love with Lila. I believe she will make me a better man. A man worthy of Arthur's friendship. My place at the round table would be earned rather than granted by the request of kin.

But if I do not do her bidding, I will lose both the girl and the king's favor. I remember when I was first enamored of Natheria. Her dark hair and creamy skin were a great attraction. In those days I was enchanted by her looks and further enticed by her power. A power I wanted for myself, and yet the more I long for Lila the less entrancing does Natheria become. So with a heavy heart I went to the castle in search of a torch.

When I returned I saw Natheria on her knees beside the bog, drawing dead leaves over the bank of the mire. She lifted her head and motioned for me to bring the torch. I looked around hoping that no one was present that would notice our nefarious activities.

She had in her hand a stone and was striking her knife against it to create a spark. It ignited and she set the leaves to burn. Taking the torch from me, rather abruptly, she ignited the pitch.

It was becoming clear to me that she no longer trusted me implicitly, as she had in the past. I would have to do something to restore her trust.

"Mistress, how is this going to help us achieve our goal?"

"Percy, you really are a dolt. We are going to start a fire, the like of which you have never seen."

"And how is that going to get us the incantation?"

"Trust me, oh foolish one, they will scramble like rats from a sinking ship. Lila will rush to the sanctuary to save the scriptures and the others will be so concerned with the fire they will not notice her."

"I see what is it you want me to do? Do I encircle the bog with the torch?"

"There is no need for that, remember the fuse? I don't want to risk you being seen. You must be very careful of the fuse line. It crosses back upon itself and if you move it only slightly, the entire area, bog, church, and wood will be devoured as if swallowed by a massive fire-breathing dragon. This is a carefully planned operation, there is no time for daydreaming or dawdling." I'm sure it is not my person she fears revealed, all she cares about is her plan not being foiled. I still marvel how I am so easily attracted to her.

Perhaps Natheria is right. I am a dolt.

"Listen closely, Percival, once the panic ensues I want you to capture the church girl and let her believe you are taking her to safety on Sir Bors orders. You are to convince her she is in no danger and that you have seen the error of your ways. Enforce upon her that fact that you have returned to my brother's company. Be meek and contrite. She must trust you are to be her savior. Signal my men. They have their orders they will know what to do."

BLACK DUFF

I smelt the faint scent of burning wood. Not aged timber, but green wood. It sputtered for several minutes and then caught aflame to older wood. The fire was building fast. The vines of the church were burning at an alarming rate. I ran to Sir Bors.

"Bors, I fear the church is afire. We must do something to save it."

I could tell from the expression on his face, he, too, perceived the danger. "Men," he called out, "Form a bucket brigade we have to contain this fire or it will take not only the church but the entire wood as well."

In a matter of minutes, a fast-moving line formed, each man using the oat bin he used to feed his horse. A complete line returned the buckets from the nearby bog. Once the buckets were poured onto the fire the conflagration rose higher and higher. The men were so intent on their task they did not notice the rising flames until I cried out, "Stop! The liquid is flammable. It is making the destruction worse."

The men quickly halted and began screaming. Their hands were blistering as the caustic substance ate away at their skin. Seasoned knights who had endured many manners of torture were brought low by this flesh- eating monster. The skin was seared and melted like wax. Their cries of agony would break the heart of the most stoic of men.

It was then I noticed both Lila and my sister running into the burning church. Lila screaming she must save the holy book and Natheria throwing herself at the pedestal where the cross once stood. Lila emerged with the sacred book, her face blackened with soot and there were thin ribbons of sparks on her shoes. Quickly she stamped them out and clutched even tighter to the book she felt was worth risking her life for, but Natheria remained within. I screamed over the roaring fire, "Natheria, you must come out. You will surely die."

"No, no. If the church is gone, there will be no magic. I must save the stand so the cross and stone can be put in their proper place. I want to live forever. The Priest promised." Her body was doubled in two as she coughed.

The force of the hacking wracked her body until it appeared she was shivering.

"Fool woman, if you do not come out of there you will live only moments longer." I was torn by thoughts of her evil deeds and by the equally compelling memories of my sweet little sister. I had to save her. Racing to the stream on the other side of the church, I drenched my cloak and wrapped it around my shoulders. Drawing the corner up over my head, I rushed into the blazing church. There she lay, her face blackened and her clothes covered with ash. Coughing and straining to get her breath, she clung tighter to the pedestal.

"Natty, Little Lady, let go. I will bring you to safety. I'm your hero, remember?" I lifted her as I had so many times before when she was my little sister.

She eased her hold, and then clung to my neck with the same ferocity she had as a child. I swept my cloak up and over her head and made my way through the flames. All around us burning branches fell. The conflagration raged on, devouring every flammable thing in its path.

The fluid from the bog had many strange properties. It was an accelerant, but when the foliage that made up the church was consumed, it turned to a foam that contained the fire. I'd never seen the like of it before. I wondered if the burns of the men could be healed by this foam. I hoped it might, yet feared even more greatly that it would not. Could it cause further harm or would it be the balm that erased the damage? I must advise Lila of its properties.

The burns on my sister were not caused by the bog fluid so I was certain the foam would not aid her. I turned and watched as the fire sputtered and died. Lila came up to us and bid me take the book to Arthur. "Lila, I cannot. I can't leave Natty. She needs me. I'm all the family she has.

"You are this creature's kin?"

"I'm her older brother. When our parents died, I took over her care, gradually she became more and more greedy and left to make her fortune. I searched for her for many years. Until I realized she either did not want to be found or was successful in her quest."

"Ah, I understand. Once you learned of her evil doings you abandoned your search?"

"In fact I did, but my heart could not accept she was truly out of my life. When I learned of her foul deeds, I was sickened, but still I loved the sweet little girl she once was. So you understand why I cannot leave her?" He held her close as one would a crying babe. Every tender feeling he had for his sister was apparent.

"I do, but this precious tome must be returned to Arthur at once. I am a healer as well as a Sentinel. If you take the book to Arthur I will see to your sister."

"But, Lady Lila, she is so very weak. If she should die and I was not there, I would never forgive myself. I am sorry, but please choose another to run your errand."

"Sir Duff, I understand your dilemma but fate determines you are to take the scripture to Arthur. It can be no other."

"I understand my duty to Arthur is foremost. Can I trust you to save my sister?"

"You can."

SIR BORS

This is a very strange happening. *That fire seemed controlled at first. I wonder what caused it to rage out of control?*

I turned back to the Church and noted Lila was tending someone, just outside the doors. It appeared to be a woman, but I'd just sent Gwen and Clare back to the safety of Camelot. I was certain they would go directly to Arthur.

"Lady Lila, you must move your patient farther from the church. It's not safe here."

She looked up at me, then to the church. "You're right, Sir Bors. Can you help me move Natheria?"

"Natheria? Why are you aiding her?"

"She needs my help and I am obligated to give it."

I was surprised as I lifted the lady. Though I thought her to be a formidable woman, she was in deed quite frail. As I carried her, her head lolled to the side indicating she was unconscious. I took her to the far side of the shed, where Lila made a place for her.

"Lila, have you everything you require to see to her needs?"

She nodded, and I turned my attention back to the blaze. Men were scurrying everywhere. I did not recognize all of them. *Perhaps some are from nearby cottages?*

Though the men were told to draw water only from the stream, those I did not know were tossing buckets of the flammable bog fluid. The flames again grew higher and higher. I went to confront them. As I approached, they dissipated like dew in the heat of the day. They were gone almost as if they were never there. I was prepared to send my men after them, but had no idea where to send them, I knew not even a direction. The men vanished into thin air. Totally confused, I confronted my men.

"Officer Neely, where is Black Duff?"

Neely replied somewhat hesitantly. "Ah, when I last saw him he was consoling a woman. Then Lila came to her aid and he left."

"Left? To go where?"

"I do not know, Sir. I'm certain Lila would, she was speaking to him just before he went."

This day just becomes more and more odd. Nothing so far holds any logic.

Just as I was about to believe in a stampede of unicorns, I spied Percival skulking around the shed. He moved furtively, not wanting to be observed. However, he wasn't as stealthful as I am certain he thought he was. His next step broke a large twig with a resounding snap. Looking in every direction to determine if he's been heard, all of the color drained from his face when his eyes met mine.

"Ah, Sir Bors, I did not expect to see you here. I thought you would be putting out the fire."

"Percival, I've not a care for what you thought. What are you doing here? Are you no longer in Natheria's employ? And I suggest you answer quickly and truthfully else it will be my pleasure to show you Arthur's dungeon."

"Sir Bors, I can no longer lead this duplicitous life. I know she's done many evil things, but sir, I love her."

"Who her? Natheria?"

The knight hung his head and said very softly, "Yes, Natheria."

My God, this was a knight of the King's Round Table. How can he be so enamored of this malevolent woman? "It seems to me Percival you are somewhat cavalier with your affections. I heard some of the men saying you were enchanted with Lady Lila only a week past."

"Yes, Sir, but I was trying to hide my true feelings for Natheria from myself. She made me angry, so I sought to make her jealous by paying attention to Lila."

This man was a mass of contradictions. But was he worthy of redemption? The charges against him were made by me and will not be enforceable until Arthur received my report.

I drew my sword and told him to stand fast, then ordered Neeley to bind him until we could take him to Camelot to stand trial for treason and arson. He offered no resistance and only asked he be allowed to see Natheria. He hung his head in abject contrition. Tears streamed down his face.

Given my consent, Neely took him around the corner of the shed where she lay.

Natheria was awake and raised her head smiling at him. "You caused this, you know. 'Twas you who moved the fuse with your bumbling ways. I should be furious with you, but knowing someone, anyone, actually cares for me has driven the sting from this wasp."

Could it be that fate brought these two miscreants together for a purpose?

REYNARD

I went over every inch of the church grounds. I found no lingering hot spots that might reignite. Though there was great damage, much was repairable. The altar was consumed completely, but oak was plentiful in this forest. Another piece could easily be found.

I looked to the horizon and saw a lone rider. And he was riding my Duncan. It had to be Duff, though I'd not seen him leave, he was returning from somewhere.

"Hey there, Duff, nice-looking animal you have."

"He is that, Reynard. It was my hope he would make us both rich enough that we could retire."

"Rich, eh? I like the sound of that. Have you lost faith in the concept?"

"Nay, it just seems life has a way of leading plans awry. I never thought I would again find my sister or that she'd become so vile."

"Vile? Who is your sister?" I'd been out of contact with my men and did not know Duff even had a sister.

"Natheria, and she's been badly burned trying to protect the pedestal for the cross. Lila has been tending her. I'm on my way to see her now."

"If Natheria is your sister, why would you leave if she is injured?"

"I didn't want to, but for Lila to treat her, I had to take the sacred book to Arthur."

Lila's talents seemed endless. Not only was she a sentinel, she was a healer and knew passages from the religious tome as well. She was a marvel of a woman. Furthermore, without raising a finger she'd stolen my heart.

"Well, Duff, let us she how she fares."

We approached the shed and I heard soft whimpering. A look of concern passed over Duff's features. It appeared as if he was a father worried about his only child.

"Lady Lila, how is my sister? Will she live?"

"Her burns are painful but they will heal in time. I've taken the sap of the aloe that will soothe the pain and will abate the scarring. She will require constant care for several weeks. I will stay with her, unless the King has a more qualified healer."

Her patient looked up with painful and contrite eyes. "Please, brother, I must beg your forgiveness. All I've done is take, from you, from any one I could. I'm deeply sorry. From the very depths of my soul I am truly repentant."

"Natty, you're forgiven. I'm sure God has already forgiven you and I have as well. Now, sleep. Your only task now is to heal."

While I sympathize with Duff, all my attention is drawn to the beautiful Lila.

"Lila, how is it you are not burned?" Her skin was as unblemished as a newborn babe was.

"I'm not sure. When I went into the church, I was hit with the bog liquid and it burned with the worst pain I've ever felt. The pain nearly knocked me senseless. Then as I gathered the sacred book, the fluid bubbled and became slippery. I fell, and wherever the bubbles touched, my skin was healed."

It was clearly a miracle. Her faith has saved her. *Oh, that I could have such trust that would allow me to remain a man and marry the woman I love.* As I stared at her, I swear my breath was stolen. That she was my soul mate was truth without question. She smiled, and I knew she felt the same.

We would be together. It was my fondest dream, come true.

Epilogue

As time touches our lives, the hard edges are softened. The hurts are forgotten and those who live well prosper.

Amadeaus is restored to his former position and Lila assists him with his church duties.

Natheria and Sir Percival scour the land for lost church manuscripts. Sir Reynard and Sir Duff raise warhorses of such a quality they are renown throughout the known world.

GWEN

"Oh, Arthur, isn't this grand? Our church has been restored and today we have three couples being wed."

"Yes, Gwen, my pet, today the beauty of your Green Cathedral will shine as I once imagined it for you."

"I know. And did you ever believe Sir Bors would marry?"

"Well, he's always been faithful to his duties. I'm certain he will be the husband Clare deserves."

I quickly turned as I heard the rustling of gowns. I would be hard pressed to choose the most beautiful. Even Natty was resplendent alongside of Sir Percival. Love had softened her. She was truly a stunning woman.

I felt my husband's arm around my waist and looked up at him.

"I know what you are thinking, Gwen. While the ladies are all very lovely, you are the fairest in my eyes."

I am the most fortunate of women. For as foolish as I have been he's forgiven me and loves me still. I wish all three couples the same joy.

My dress is simple, but my seamstresses labored long to create the masterpieces the three brides wore.

Amadeaus stood solemnly at the end of the long aisle. As each pair approached, he directed them to their position. Natty and Sir Percival to his left, Sir Bors and Clare to his right, and Sir Reynard, and Lady Lila directly in front of him.

Sir Duff stood beside the men as the best man and I served as matron of honor to the ladies. I'd never before seen such a spectacular wedding. Truly a magical moment.

Now, dear readers, if you are wondering about Sir Reynard becoming a fox again, fear not, for he has learned to control his temper.

Also from **Dee Carey** and **Writers' Branding:**

FOX TALES

Two Tales of Love Mark of the Fox

Can an enchanted fox and a scarred prince follow the predestined course the Druids have set for them? They fight against the constraints of royalty, but in the end the falconer becomes a willing regent and the fox, his more- than-willing wife.

The Fox and the Swan

To save her family, a girl becomes a swan. The man she loves is enchanted by a witch into a fox. Can the pair unite as humans and save her family? True love triumphs over evil with the aid of a druid, a bishop, and a goddess.
Available now on Amazon.

THE CRIMSON VIXEN

The preordained couple meet when Leigh discovers an orphaned fox and keeps her as a secret companion. In time it is revealed his Kit is also a fierce female pirate. The Druids determine the pair are destined to rule Ireland. As a fox she is clever. As a woman she is enchanting. Can Leigh set aside his devotion to King Arthur to be with the woman of his dreams?
Available now on Amazon.

FOX TALES II

Two tales will enchant and bring to you the joy of magic, faith, courage, and the most powerful force in the universe: Love.
Can Sean save himself and his friends from the grasp of the most foul?
Can Merlot and LaRoux follow their preordained paths to save church and country?
Available now on Amazon.

www.ingramcontent.com/pod-product-compliance
Lightning Source LLC
LaVergne TN
LVHW041539060526
838200LV00037B/1048